The Alchemist's Rose

R. S. Parker

To Donna B., a doll of a doll

1

"Yes, Mom, I understand the situation, but I'm in the middle of writing my dissertation. The semester's just about to start. I can't just up and leave." Sara glanced at the clock on her computer. "Shit! We can talk later, Mom, but I'm about to be late for a meeting with Professor Hayes-Grey."

"I'll make you this deal, Sara, and then I'll let you go. If you do this, we'll pay for the rest of your studies and buy you a new car."

"Fine, Mom. I've got to go. Love you. Bye."

With a heavy exhalation, Sara cradled her face in her own right hand. She ground her teeth and grumbled. This wasn't needed right now. Two chapters remained on her dissertation, and, if she wanted to graduate at the end of the spring semester, she needed to have the chapters completed by January. This should be easy to do—even with this setback.

Sara's breath came in deep, swift pants. *What am I going to do? I don't need this right now. I've got enough bullshit. I'm going to lose everything. I won't get my degree. My family will lose the money we've apparently been using to live off of for most of my life. Why? Why should I pack up and move to some town in Pennsylvania I've never heard of. Didn't even know my great grandfather was still alive. It's not like we ever met. And why does the stipulation include marriage—and to a man? Poop! I'm going to disappoint Professor Hayes-Grey like I disappoint my family.*

With a final sigh, she nodded and then rose from her chair. *Let's get moving.*

She took note of everything in the office she shared with Andrea Jones-Cook as she walked to the door. Most children had larger bedrooms dedicated to a single occupant, but two adults shared this white-walled space for grading, working, and meeting with students. hastily patched ceiling revealed where squirrels and rats burrowed their way through the structure. Two rusted iron desks sat atop cracked tiles near the back wall. With the semester just starting, both desks showed the promise of organization. Color-coded and labeled file boxes joined with framed family photos on Andrea's desk, and Sara had straightened the stack of printed journal articles atop her own. The hallway on the office floor for History and English teaching assistants was long and narrow. Undergraduate students joked that it resembled a scene from a horror movie. Rectangular shrouds containing fluorescent lights that flickered unevenly clung to the ceiling, and the dingy white tiles on the floor were cracked and broken. Half of the bulbs needed replacement, causing long, uneven shadows to stretch over the hall. With the office doors closed, no sound traveled into the hallway, and footsteps echoed in uneven patterns. The air was always cold and reeked of stale bread and mold.

Halfway down the stairs between the third and second floors, Sara passed Andrea Jones-Cook on the way up to their office. They hugged and kissed each other's cheeks. Andrea was three inches taller than Sara, and her long, lustrous black curls fell to the small of her back. Brown eyes shone from behind her round, wire-rimmed glasses. When she smiled, the height of her cheekbones became clearly visible, and her chocolate brown lipstick drew out the warm undertones of her olive skin. She appeared to be about Sara's age but was a full decade older. "Sorry to run, Drea," Sara said. "I'm about to be late to my meeting with Professor Hayes-Grey."

Andrea raised a canvas tote bag filled with books, papers, and binders. "I'm only heading up to drop this off before my meeting Professor Alliveri. We'll catch up later. You're coming to my *Welcome to the Semester's Fresh Hell* party next Friday, right?"

Sara shook her head. "Don't think so. I may be packing up to move by then. Family stuff. I'll fill you in later. Meet me for drinks at The Dervish tomorrow?"

Andrea sighed. "I'm sorry. I know how your family is. We'll miss you. No one gets a dance floor started with karaoke quite like you. But yeah, around six tomorrow? Well, good luck in the meeting."

Sara smiled. "See you tomorrow. And, hey, you too."

They parted ways. Sara smiled as she descended to the second floor. The eastern hallway on the second floor of Edward Talbot Hall. Rows of mahogany Gothic arches, interspersed with doors leading to classrooms and faculty offices, rose to the middle of the white stone walls. Tiling designed to mimic the appearance of the old wooden floors gleamed from a fresh pre-semester polishing. Through the half-opened doors of professors' offices, a cacophony of sounds emerged. Professor Hendricks was listening to *The Pirates of Penzance*. Professor Astor-Jones had older episodes of *Nexus Adventures*, a *Dungeons & Dragons* actual play game livestreamed on Twitch and YouTube playing in her office. And Professor Hayes-Grey had an environmental activist podcast, *Earth First*, playing in hers.

Sara knocked three times and waited. Her dissertation chair paused the podcast and said, "Come in."

Sara opened the door and walked inside. Sitting behind her massive mahogany desk with her back to the large window that overlooked the University Commons, Professor Alexandra Hayes-Grey returned Sara's smile as her advisee sat in the wooden chair in front of her. A wall of shelves filled with academic texts on theory and various research subjects connected to the history of eating habits, environmentalism in Louisiana, and the history of science and medicine filled the shelves. The tenured professor's leathered hands and the crisp, starched cuffs of her white Oxford-style blouse poked out from her blue, green, and gray tweed jacket. A handful of bluish wisps of hair mixed with the silver curls that framed her long, narrow face. Her once-fair skin had developed a ruddy tan from summers spent in the garden, but her green eyes sparkled with the youthfulness of early middle age. Steam rose from the brown *Campus Roasters* cup beside her right hand.

"Good afternoon, Professor." Sara said. "Thank you for meeting with me today. How was your summer?"

"Filled with much work, as yours seems to have been." Professor Hayes-Grey patted the massive stack of papers on her desk. "And I received your email this morning. "I'm sorry for your loss."

Sara nodded. "I appreciate it. I didn't know my great grandfather, but there's some stuff about his passing that we'll talk about later. So, you read my latest draft?"

"You're writing is elegant, fluid, and beautiful as always, Sara. Your research is deep, thorough, and, overall, persuasive. No surprise there." Professor Hayes-Grey's honest but hesitant words crept from her mouth. Her voice faltered at the end.

"Thank you, Professor Hayes-Grey, but I sense a *but* coming," Sara said, her alto voice faltered through her smile. Her lungs clutched the next breath tightly, and her muscles tensed.

Sara Alexander sat on the opposite side of her dissertation chair's mahogany desk. Far younger than her adviser, Sara kept her blonde hair in a chin-length asymmetrical bob that framed her round, tanned face. Her emerald eyes darkened as she looked over the frames of her vintage-inspired half-moon eyeglasses. The collar of her cream blouse peeked out from behind the safety of her burgundy cardigan. Her manicured fingers fidgeted with the hem of her green and gray plaid skirt.

Professor Hayes-Grey nodded, offering a heavy sigh. "You know what I'm about to say, Sara," she said. She sipped the café au lait that had grown cold. "The argument you put forth in chapter four, where you suggest that Samuel Hahnemann's homeopathic thesis would have been applicable to mental illness, as he technically proposed in his diary—which you cited appropriately and liberally—but stated it required a *tincturam magnae animae*, alleged to be present in the Paracelsus text *De Mirabilibus Occultis Naturae*—that argument is based on tenuous but not unbelievable evidence. As I'm sure you know, this text, *De Mirabilibus*, needs to be cited directly, but you provide neither citation nor evidence of its existence beyond oblique references in decades' old scholarship."

Sara nodded. "I know I didn't cite it, but Paracelsus's treatise exists. Both Kieckeffer and Koetting cite it in their works on the history of Renaissance and Enlightenment alchemy in Europe. I just haven't been able to get my hands on it yet."

The professor shook her head. "Sara, you can't submit a draft with a glaring omission like that. You're better than that. Have you tried our Interlibrary Loan Office?"

An exasperated sigh rumbled through Sara's lips. She ran her fingers through her hair. She shook her head. "They couldn't find it. I emailed Koetting, and they said they found in a private collection. They transcribed the pages they needed, and they can attest to its legitimacy."

Professor Hayes-Grey leaned forward. She rubbed the bridge of her nose with the thumb and index finger of her right hand. She released a long, slow breath. "I was hoping you wouldn't say that. No, don't argue right now, Sara. You're a bright, talented scholar. You're one of the more decorated doctoral candidates we've taught in the past twenty years, but this isn't the Seventies. Academia has changed. Expectations are higher. Time requirements are stricter. You know where I'm going with this?"

Sara slammed her fist on the desk and nodded. "I know, Professor. I have that. I just need to get my hands on the *De Mirabilibus*, and then I'm—"

Professor Hayes-Grey extended her open hand to silence her advisee. She offered a sympathetic smile in response to Sara's defeated expression. "I'm on your side. I petitioned for your fifth year because I believe in your passion and your work."

Sara threw her hands up. "What do you want me to do? I know I'm right on this, and if we can reproduce this tincture, perhaps we could help so many suffering people."

"There's being right, and there's being finished. College funding is tied to completion rates. The Board of Directors is now pushing for completion in four years. To that end, a new policy went into effect at the start of August, limiting funding to four years for students pursuing doctoral degrees and limiting colleges to enough funds for only a handful of fifth-year students."

"Great, so I'm on my own or out in May then." The words grumbled through Sara's lips as she snorted in annoyance.

"I didn't say that," her dissertation chair said. "Perhaps we can grandfather you in, since you were well into your program of study when this policy will go into effect. However, you will need the support of the majority of our faculty for a sixth year petition to have any hope of success."

A relieved sigh slid through Sara's lips. Her body relaxed in the mahogany chair, and she smiled. "At least most of them like me, and I think those that don't at least respect my work."

"They do."

"There is another option, Sara. You could rework your argument so this source isn't needed. That would allow you to finish drafting this semester, defend in January, and graduate in May. It's a good bit of work, but you're smart and talented. If you dedicate yourself, you can do it."

Sara nodded. Her gaze shifted from Professor Hayes-Grey to the window behind her. The second-floor office overlooked the University Commons, and the last azalea blooms of the season decorated the green with fragrant pink, yellow, and orange blossoms. Autumn was around the corner for the city of Nouvelle Arniers. A new topic, a literature review, and two chapters of analysis in six—maybe seven—weeks was a tall order. She sighed.

Sara ran her fingers through her hair and scratched behind her ear. "Neither of these are going to be easy, are they?"

"Nothing worth doing ever is." Professor Hayes-Grey pushed the dissertation draft, bloodied with her comments and edits, toward Sara. "Look, I know you've had a few family struggles and recent events haven't made things any easier for you. I can see it in your face, struggling to keep your natural smile in place for the world to see. It's okay to admit you're struggling."

"I'm fine, but thank you." Sara placed the pages inside her chestnut brown leather laptop bag alongside her laptop. Thank you for your time, Professor." Sara rose and moved to leave Professor Hayes-Grey' office. When her hand touched the doorknob, she paused. "Oh, one more thing, Professor. About my great grandfather's passing. In his will there's a provision that requires me to take possession of his home in some town in Pennsylvania and live there or everyone loses the money and possessions they're set to inherit. It's stupid, but I have to do this for my family. Will that be okay?"

Professor Hayes-Grey closed her eyes and nodded. "Life never happens when it's convenient, does it? You started your studies right before the pandemic started, so you know we have the infrastructure for remote work. Talk to Donna and Loretta about your assistantship. The semester just began, so there may be time to switch your classes from traditional to virtual classes. There's no guarantee, but you can at least continue your research remotely."

A weak but honest smile graced Sara's lips. She nodded. "Thank you, Professor. I'm looking forward to being closer to New York and its libraries, but it's neither the best situation or timing. Have a nice day."

Sara Alexander exited her dissertation chair's office.

Sara's cobalt blue Honda Civic sputtered as she pulled into the parking lot of the Bienville Court Towne Homes. The motion sensor controlling the wrought iron gate was broken again, leaving the gate in a perpetual open state. The complex's three buildings resembled rows of brownstone houses arranged around a central common area with pools, a series of charcoal grills, and patio furniture around a fire pit. Sara parked her car and checked the mailbox, grabbing the university notices, coupon circular, and half a dozen unwanted pre-approved credit card and payday loan applications. Buried behind that clutter, she found a lavender envelope containing a card addressed to her roommate. Sara tossed the junk in the trash bin and headed to her townhouse.

Unit B-11 was in the middle of the northern building. Sara unlocked the door and stepped into the small foyer. Closing the door behind her, she said, "Candace, a card came for you!"

No one answered. Sara shrugged and placed the card upright in the basket marked *Mail* on the side. She passed the den. A purple, green, and blue plaid sofa and a maple coffee table stood out against the cream walls. The ascending staircase was on her left. After that, she passed the stairs that descended to the basement, and then she arrived at the unit's kitchen and pantry.

Sara set her purse, laptop case, and books on the small dining table next to the island. She groaned and rubbed the back of her neck. Sara walked to the stainless steel refrigerator and saw a note Candace left her on the dry erase board.

Sara, had to go into work at two. Grabbed the hummus and veg to snack on while working. Sorry! I'll buy you more tomorrow. Should be home around two in the morning. See you tomorrow!

A sound between a whine and a growl stumbled from Sara's lips. She grabbed her cell phone and opened her GrubHub app. "Well," she said, "Time for delivery."

Forty-three minutes later, the Ali Baba's Mediterranean Restaurant delivery driver brought Sara's stuffed grape leaves, falafel, hummus with pita bread for dipping, and baklava. Sara used that time to undress, remove her makeup, and change into her oversized teal hoodie and gray pajama pants.

Sara popped one stuffed grape leaf into her mouth. As she chewed, she opened apps for both Tumblr and Deviant Art. On the latter site, someone named Wencidluvvr sent a message asking her rate on six or eight illustrations for a seventy-thousand-word fanfic she wrote over the summer. Flattered, Sara browsed rate cards for artists who did similar stylistic work for ideas on how to price her work. While searching, the *ba ding* alerting her that she had received a new email sounded.

Sara switched browser tabs back to her email. She sighed. Her mother had already booked a moving company, Cows Can Steer Movers, to assist her in getting to Pazat, Pennsylvania. She left next Thursday.

"Well, I'm done for the night," Sara said, "Might as well do something where I have control."

Sara shoved her cell phone in the hoodie's pocket. Rising from the table, she walked into their den and curled up on the couch.

She grabbed the white Xbox controller and powered on the console. When *Stardew Valley* opened automatically, Sara shook her head. Calming, yes, but the tale of a young person who moves to a small town after elderly relative dies hit too close to home. *Hellblade: Senua's Sacrifice* had the action and ambiance she desired, but its pacing was too languid. Shaking her head, she switched from her Xbox to her Switch and booted up *Bayonetta 3*.

Sara licked her lips. "Time for some exploitation gaming action."

With her phone still on silent while immersed in the bright, fast-paced gun-and-magic action as Bayonetta kicked, hair-whipped, and blasted her way through hordes of enemies. In the hours before dawn, Candace Arbuncle returned home from work. Her brown hair fell from the messy bun, and her cobalt scrubs had a handful of stains on them. Hearing her friend and roommate produce a thunderous belch while gaming, she grabbed a water bottle from the refrigerator, walked to the den, and said, "Didn't expect you to wait up for me, Dad."

Sara stiffened and squeaked. She spun around before pausing, spun back, checked her phone, and then exited the game. "Damn, I didn't realize it was after three in the morning." She yawned and then offered Candace a sheepish but genuine grin. "How was the ER, Doc?"

Candace drained half of the water bottle in a series of gulps before sitting on the sofa beside Sara. She gestured to her scrubs and said, "Bloody, barfy, and pissy. Just another night, and before you ask, no one came in with anything interesting up their asses. I miss anything on your end of town?"

Sara yawned. "Looks like I'm going to finish my dissertation remotely. That's all."

Candace felt Sara's forehead. "You don't feel like you have a fever. What symptoms are you experiencing? Cough? Fatigue? Mental confusion? Dizziness?"

With a dismissive hand, Sara said, "I'm fine, physically at least. No, Mom's already hired movers to pack my stuff and help me move to Pazat, Pennsylvania, next Thursday."

"Moving? Why?" Candace sipped the water.

Sara rolled her eyes. She sighed. "Remember when she called to tell me my great grandfather, Danforth Julian Alexander the Fourth, died? Well, the will was read, and apparently, he's been sending my parents the money we've been living on for the last twenty years, and there's a provision in the will that those payments will stop if I don't go to that town, live in his old house, and marry an acceptable man. I have three years to complete that last bit, so, there's that."

Candace winced. "That sucks—more for you than for me. I guess there's no footnote saying an acceptable woman is acceptable?"

Sara blew a raspberry at the ceiling. She shook her head. "No"

"Damn. I'll miss you, but I understand." She yawned. "We'll plan your going away party later, but we both need sleep."

Sara nodded. "Yeah. Sleep sounds good."

August in Louisiana was the perfect time to remain indoors. The subtropical climate brought beautiful sunshine and long days in the summer along with oppressive temperatures and mosquito swarms anytime standing water forms in ditches, yards, parking lots, or even potholes. Rain brought not relief but instead a thickening of the air with a moist soupiness that clung to and weighed down any clothing worn.

On this particular Saturday morning in August, Sara skipped her morning run, choosing instead to sleep late. After a quick breakfast of impossible sausage, toast, and grape jam paired with a strawberry protein shake, Sara donned her athletic wear, packed a duffel bag with casual wear, and headed to the St. Albertus Magnus Recreation Center for a five-mile run and some strength training. After her shower, she changed into a cream modernized poet shirt with handkerchief cuffs and a fitted waistcoat and trousers in a British khaki with camel pinstripes before grabbing a quick lunch at Seed Organic Vegan Café.

She returned to her townhouse and sat on her queen bed. The cream lace canopy she hung from the ceiling fluttered in the air conditioner's whirring breeze. Her burgundy comforter with an embroidered pattern of golden fleur-de-lis lay crumpled at the corner of the bed, revealing the cream sheets beneath it. Four pillows, two burgundy and two cream, lay stacked against the mahogany headboard, and Sara's collection of vintage-style, velveteen stuffed animals with button eyes rested on the pillows. The pink Acer laptop clashed stylistically with the fountain pens, burgundy eternal rose in a glass case, the floral teacup in which Sara drank her coffee, and the brown leather-bound journal sitting atop her antique mahogany writing desk with the matching three-shelf bookcase standing at its left. Cream lace curtains hovered before the window behind the desk. Framed drawings of Sara's in various sizes, mostly portraits of family, friends, and the occasional landscape adorned the walls.

A growling sigh rumbled from Sara's lips as she surveyed her room. "I don't like strangers going through my things, so let's see how much I can get packed. Everything in here is going, that's for sure. Great-grandfather might have an even nicer bed, but I'm not sleeping on a stranger's mattress—even if it's bigger than mine. I can pack my books, my art, and most of my clothes. I'm only teaching on Tuesday and Thursday, so I'll only need four outfits and my workout gear. Maybe I'll keep five out, just in case. I'll pack my knick-knacks and trinkets today, but my bedding will wait until Thursday morning. I'll leave all the furniture in the den and dining room that's mine for Candace. I don't want to do this."

She set the alarm on her phone and then started organizing. She made a note to pick up boxes tomorrow, but today she grouped her possessions into piles by necessity over the next week. She planned her outfits for the week and set them aside. Then, she folded the remaining clothing when appropriate and packed everything else in her suitcases, suit bags, and dress bags. The stuffed animals would wait until closer to time, as Sara didn't want to sleep without them. When her alarm sounded, she grabbed the brown leather backpack she used as a casual purse and headed out the door.

The Dervish was a campus bar without being a campus bar. It sat just far enough away from campus, had slightly higher prices, and a notable lack of the more common, low-end alcohol so as to keep away underage students trying to sneak into a bar. Its patio resembled the courtyard of a Florentine villa with wrought iron tables and chairs around a central fountain where a dervish danced amidst the gurgling of the water. The interior had electric candles atop the mahogany tables and electric sconces protruding from the wooden panels of the walls. The moody lighting paired well with the soft jazz played over the speakers during the week and by the live band, usually the Benji Simmons Trio, on the weekend. All the furniture was mahogany and brown leather. The Dervish was clean, classy, and quiet enough for a conversation. Graduate students and younger professors loved the place.

With the semester starting on Wednesday of the following week, the bar was half full. Sara grabbed an empty seat at the bar while she waited for Andrea to arrive. After a minute, the bartender, a stunning black woman with a shaved head, a strong jaw, and high cheek bones accentuated with golden highlighter approached. Sara's jaw dropped. "Pru? When did you start working here?"

Pru, or Prudence Sturm, smiled. She wore emerald lipstick. "Started this week. Before you ask, I'm still at the Green Faerie, but I'm picking up a shift or two here each week. What brings you into my bar this evening?"

"Meeting a friend for drinks, explaining why I'm moving. That type of thing."

Pru jerked her head back and blinked. "Moving? Getting a new place?"

Sara shook her head. "Leaving the state. Long story short, some stupid condition of my dead great grandfather's will is that I move into his old house in Pennsylvania and then live there while looking for a husband. Otherwise, my parents lose all the money he gives them each month."

Prudence whistled. "Shit, that's rough. I'm sorry, Sara. First one's on the house. What do you want?"

Sara shook her head. "No, I'm paying you for it. Gin and tonic."

"Be back in a flash."

Prudence walked to the center of the bar and mixed the drink. She kept an eye on Sara, and when the blonde turned her back, Prudence doubled the pour. She knew Sara would pay her and would tip at least fifty percent of her bar tab, so she wanted to offer a little liquid sympathy. She returned with the drink and set it atop a napkin. Sara handed Prudence her debit card, which Prudence scanned and returned before slipping away to tend to another customer.

Ten minutes passed before Andrea arrived. She styled her hair into a messy bun and wore a fitted black and white striped tee tucked into dark wash, boot cut jeans. After a quick hug and cheek kisses, she sat on the stool beside Sara and ordered a glass of Sangiovese wine.

After Prudence brought the wine and a round of just-in-case waters, Andrea asked, "So, what's going on that's got you off your game? You mentioned something about your family?"

Sara sipped her drink and nodded. "Yeah. I think I mentioned to you earlier in the week that my great grandfather died. If not, he died of old age. We'll circle back to that, but first, it seems that my great grandfather—my mom's grandfather—has been using his wealth so my parents could keep up the appearance of wealth when a bunch of crap went down with my dad when I was a kid. He's been supplying my family with like almost all the money we've had for twenty years now. Anyway, his will has been read, and there's a stipulation that says if I don't move into his house and within three years marry a suitable man..." Sara paused to roll her eyes and drain her gin and tonic before continuing. "Well, that's then all the money dries up. I leave one week from Thursday. Mom has so kindly hired movers to pack and transport my stuff."

Andrea released a held breath through a slow exhale. "Damn, that's rough. So, how is this going to go with you being gay? Are you going to find a beard or just let the three years expire?"

Prudence brought Sara another drink. Sara took the first sip and then said, "I don't know how they'll take—well, I know how my parents will take—the fact that they have three years to figure things out, because I'm not marrying a man. The worst part, I'll have to miss your party, but I'm sending wine and pizza."

Andrea chuckled. "Always doing something to help Well, I'll not teaching on Thursday, so I'll help you finish packing. But what about your assistantship?"

A smile crept onto her face as Sara looked wistfully into the air. She ran her index finger around the rim of her glass. "I don't know. I'm waiting for a decision on whether my class will go remote or if I'll have to surrender the funding. I hate relying on family money, but I may have to do so. Honestly, with a big move to a new town, it may be better."

"So where are you moving to?"

"Pazat, Pennsylvania." Sara sipped her cocktail. "It's some small town in the Poconos. Never heard of it, and it barely has an Internet presence."

Andrea drained her glass. She nodded. "Interesting. Once you get settled, we'll come visit over a holiday."

Conversation turned to lighter topics and continued for another round. After that, both paid their bar tabs, tipping well, and headed home for the night.

2

Dense fog and heavy charcoal gray clouds shrouded the cool air around Pazat on this Saturday near the ides of August. Nestled at the base of the Pocono Mountains north of Honesdale in Wayne County, Pennsylvania, this small town sat at the end of a narrow, winding dirt road. Two massive farmsteads flanked the road as it entered the town. Their wood and barbed wire fences extended to the mountains surrounding the town, giving the impression a walled city.

Harvest neared, and the farmhands toiled in the fields, reaping their way through the vast seas of golden wheat with long scythes. Others plucked the vibrant red and green apples from the orchards. Other hands tended the cattle, the pigs, and the chickens. Both farms, like the other houses, had their own gardens to grow onions, peppers, garlic, and other common vegetables and herbs. 1928 Fageol trucks carried the harvested grain and produce to their destinations in and around the town.

An open air market filled the majority of the small town's square. A single church, Our Lady of Endless Mercy, stood at the eastern edge of the town's central square. The red brick town hall stood on the square's northern edge, and its architectural twin, the town school, stood on the southern edge. Other businesses surrounded the square in uneven ripples with one exception.

Skejik Toys sat at the northeastern edge of the town at the edge of the dense forest of ash, elm, and oak trees that separated Pazat from an old potter's field through a single dirt road that passed through the woods, wound around the field of unmarked and unhallowed graves, and up into the mountains, ending at the Skejik family estate. A fire reduced the original building in the town square, just south of the school, to ash decades ago, but then Radomir Blinksy's daughter Lana married Dr. Boris Skejik, and he rebuilt the store at the edge of his lands.

The shop had a spacious floor where shelves full of wooden trucks, wheeled animals on leashes, airplanes, tops, hand stitched dolls, porcelain dolls in handmade clothing, and stuffed animals. Doll houses designed after Tudor homes, Victorian town homes, and modern ranch homes sat in the windows alongside castles, forts, and armies of tin and wooden soldiers, modeled on Celtic and Norse warriors, Hessian cavalry, medieval knights and pikemen, as well as British and Colonial troops from the American Revolution. All were sculpted with a scientist's accuracy and painted without flaw. Handmade puzzles, board games, sculpted globes, and various toys designed to help toddlers and young children learn and develop skills—all painted in bright, attractive colors—sat alongside vases filled with dark purple and blue roses with star-like white specks on their petals atop the tables spaced throughout the show room.

Now that Radomir and Lana had passed on, their daughter Dobrianya managed the shop and made all of the toys, following the tradition of her mother and of her grandfather. "Anya," as her parents and their servants had called her, appeared to be in her mid-twenties. She was tall and slender with pale skin, black hair always pulled into a bun, and warm brown eyes. A scar ran the length of her face along the right side of her nose, and the area around her right eye bore scarring from a burn suffered in childhood. A black lace mourning veil shadowed her round face, and she wore a high collared, ankle-length black dress. Regardless of whether or not she wore perfume, the faint, dreamy smell of roses followed her.

Never far from Anya was her marionette Iskra. Carved by Lana when Anya was five, Iskra has been at Anya's side. The hand-carved yew marionette resembled a young girl with plaited blonde braids and realistic green eyes. She wore a gold-trimmed red vest embroidered with purple and white flowers over a white, ruffled sleeve blouse, which was tucked into a full red skirt embroidered with gold, white, and purple flowers.

The shop was empty on this Saturday afternoon, but that was to be expected on a foggy day. Children often spent those days holding lanterns for the farm hands, paid enough to afford a toy or a nice pastry for their troubles. Anya swept the floor and tidied the shelves, and Iskra sat beside the till. Her eyes stared, unblinking, at the wooden door. With the sweeping finished, Anya walked to the back room to put the broom away.

And then the door chimes sang their haunting melody. A curvy woman in her upper twenties shuffled into the store, keeping her gaze lowered. She had dusty brown hair cut short and uneven, a bulbous nose, and a plain face. She wore a red dress, white tights, and black Mary Jane shoes. The woman crossed herself as she entered the shop. Her breaths came quick and shallow. Lida's nose wrinkled at the faint, almost dreamy, smell of distant roses that permeated the store filled her nose.

As the woman browsed the dolls along the wall, Iskra's nasal soprano voice sounded through the store. "We've got a customer! Oh, it's Lida Petska."

Lida squealed at Iskra's words. Her eyes darted about the store, and she stuttered her words as she said, "Oh, hi, Iskra. Is…" She stiffened as Anya silently emerged from the back room. For the briefest of moments, Lida made eye contact with Anya's glare, but she raised her hand to shield her eyes She added, "Oh, there she is—there you scar—I mean, there you are. How do you do that?"

Anya nodded without saying a word. The subtle scent of roses intensified in Lida's nose as Anya glided over to the till, scooped up Iskra, and then walked to stand before Lida, who stood half a foot shorter than the toymaker did. She sneezed, and her eyes watered. Pressure built around her nose, cheeks, and forehead.

Iskra's voice cut the fog of silence. "So, Petska Wetska, looking for a dolly and some dry sheets?"

Lida walked to the wall and took one of the cotton, velveteen, and burlap rag dolls with braided hair of golden yarn. The seams were flawless, and the fabrics provided pleasant contrasts of textures. The yarn's softness felt like human hair. Lida clutched the doll tight against her chest. Her breathing slowed, and a smile slid across her face.

"Please don't call me that, Iskra." Lida's speech was languid and airy. "I haven't wet myself since school. I came to buy a doll. Carolyn wants a doll to give one to Elisa, since her sister Danika was chosen to be the Dożynki maiden. I always wanted to lead the procession from the fields to the church, but I was too plain and my family too poor, unlike Carolyn. What about you, Anya? Did you ever want to lead the procession?"

Anya shook her head and squeezed Iskra's strings, preventing her head and mouth from telling a different story with its movements. Once she was quieted, Anya selected a porcelain doll from the top shelf. The doll had strawberry blonde silken ribbons curled into springy ringlets. Anya offered Lida the porcelain doll, and the shorter woman shuffled her purse and the other doll around as she accepted this new doll. The doll's head turned and winked at Iskra. Lida's arms closed defensively, but at Anya's insistence, Lida accepted the doll.

While Lida appraised the craftsmanship, Iskra said, "Anya can easily sculpt a new face to look like the whiny little—" Anya jerked the marionette's strings, causing Iskra to sputter in surprise. Iskra glared at Anya but then turned her attention back to Lida and said, "Anya can make the doll look like the little angel. She could have it done by Monday, and it would only cost twenty dollars more."

Lida thought for a moment. Her eyes unfocused for a brief instant, and when they refocused, the porcelain doll's face resembled Elisa's chubby but rosy cheeks, crooked smile with uneven teeth, and her chunky strawberry blonde bangs that regularly poked the child in her almond-shaped green eyes. Lida smiled, and the doll seemed to smile back and giggle. After a trio of sneezes, Lida blinked, and the doll's features returned to their original form, masterful and realistic but indistinct.

Nodding and yawning, Lida said, "That seems like a good plan. Yes, I think Carolyn would want me to do that. Oh, and I'll take this rag doll too. I like her."

Anya nodded. With a gesture by both Iskra and herself, Anya guided Lida to the register. Lida placed the porcelain doll beside the register. As Anya pushed the buttons on the antique device, Iskra said, "Well, that will be fifteen for the rag doll, and fifty-five for the porcelain doll dressed as the Dożynki maiden plus an extra twenty for the rush custom job. You need to pay for the rag doll and half of the porcelain doll now, and the remainder of it when you pick it up on Monday. So, today, your grand total will be fifty-two dollars and fifty cents with thirty-seven dollars and fifty cents due on Monday."

Anya wrapped the rag doll in pink and white tissue paper and placed it inside an ornate wooden box that bore the moniker of Blinsky Toys, *There is no fun where there is no Blinsky*. She tied a bow from strands of pink and white ribbon over the box's center point. Lida thought for a moment, checking her green and red plaid coin purse. She frowned and sighed. That was more than she planned on paying, but Carolyn told—no, *asked*—her to do this. She nodded and handed over the money. "That seems fair."

Iskra snatched the money from Lida's hand, and Anya handed Lida the boxed and wrapped rag doll. Lida's eyes watered, but she offered Anya a faint smile. "Thank you, Anya. It's always a pleasure—er, it's nice—to do business with you. Well, I'll see you at the festival. Bye."

Lida scurried out the door. The chimes sang their haunting tune. As the door shut behind her, Iskra said, "Goodbye, Petska

Wetska! Hope that doll teaches you how to change your diapers."

Anya shushed Iskra. Her voice was a gentle and faltering mezzo soprano. "Don't say that. It will cause trouble, and I don't want that."

Iskra waved a dismissive hand. "She's harmless. What's she going to do? Tell that uppity bitch Carolyn Ward I was mean to her? That I called her names?" Iskra threw her head back and cackled. "Anyway, it's time to close shop and go home for the weekend."

Anya nodded. She began counting the money in the till, chatting idly with Iskra. As Anya finished the count, the door chimes sang their melancholic song. Anya and Iskra both focused their gaze on the young girl who scurried into the store and ducked behind one of the display tables, wrapping her arms around her scuffed knees as she panted and wheezed. Anya walked over and kneeled beside the young girl.

"What's wrong, little one," she asked.

The young girl sniffed, sucking snot into her nose. When she lifted her tear-filled, brown eyes, blood trickled from the scrape on her fair forehead. Anya wiped the girl's forehead with a monogrammed handkerchief. The girl looked no older than eight, and her chestnut brown hair was styled in a braided ponytail. The faint smell of feces emanated from her feet. There was a brown lump on her left Mary Jane. Anya nodded, offering the girl a kind smile from behind her veil.

The girl's jaw trembled, and her voice stuttered and cracked as she said, "I'm sorry, Miss Skejik. Bobby Kramar and Milos Ward pushed me down the steps in front of church, calling me

Darva Dookie because I didn't notice dog poopie on the stairs. Then they threw rocks at me, and I ran."

Anya heard her own heart thunder once in her chest. Her eyes grew distant, and memories flooded her mind. Chased into the girls' restroom at the town's school, her tormentors banged on the stall door and laughed as they dumped buckets of fish, animal feces, and dirty water onto her head as she cried and begged them to stop. Anya's hands trembled, and she swallowed hard.

Iskra turned her gaze toward the store windows. "I don't see the little shit stirrers. Let them come over here. I'll show them the pain of my wooden shoes!"

Anya snapped to the present. She nodded. "They may not have chased you here, little one, but we will be careful, yes? Why don't you wait here while I finish closing my shop? Then you can slip out the back door and skirt the edge of the forest, no?"

"I—are you sure?" The girl's eyes were glassy.

Anya wiped the fecal matter from the girl's shoe. They would need washing, but this was what she could do. Rising, Anya walked to the door. She opened the door and surveyed the foggy cobblestone street in front of her shop. No children's forms were visible through the fog. She closed the door and locked it.

Turning her attention back to the young girl, Anya said, "I am, little one. We will not be much longer." She extended a hand to the child. "While you wait, why not pick a single toy you can carry with you?"

The girl's eyes widened, and her broad smile revealed the gap between her front teeth. "You mean it?"

Anya nodded. The girl took her hand and walked around the store. She selected a plush golden retriever, which she named Angelica. Once the closing process was finished, Anya and Iskra escorted the child out of the shop through the rear door. They watched as she slipped into the woods and moved back toward the town. Once they could no longer see her, they walked the path toward the Skejik manor.

The forest trail had narrowed in the years since Boris and Lana had passed. While it was once wide and smooth enough for an automobile to drive with minimal difficulty, the 1938 Rolls Royce Wraith has remained entombed in the manor's carriage house since Mikhail Gonshorev passed away during the winter of Anya's sixteenth year. During inclement weather, Anya traveled by the family's old carriage, pulled by a pair of black marionette horses Anya designed out of necessity. She received no visitors at the manor, and none ventured beyond the potter's field. As a result, the forest had reclaimed much of the trail, leaving only a gnarled and narrow path, overgrown with grass, weed, and tree roots. Ash and elm trees with low branches that grasped at those who walked along the path's edge.

On this Saturday, Anya carried Iskra in her arms as they walked home. Having passed the potter's field, the day's fog limited visibility to six steps ahead. The kitten heels on Anya's laced ankle boots crunched grass, twigs, and fallen leaves beneath them. Birds whistled and sang in the trees, and crickets chirped while a massive ten-point whitetail buck froze and stared, his eyes following Anya as she walked along the path. The dreamy floral scent of roses, violets, and wildflowers cut through the thick woodsy scent of the forest.

"I don't know why we couldn't take the carriage," Iskra said. "The fog is making my clothes all damp, and it's not good for my joints either."

"Most days at the end of summer and through the autumn are foggy, Iskra. If the dampness is bad for your joints, think what it would do to the horses. I hope that young girl made it home safely."

Iskra nodded. "We could have followed her home to make sure. There's still plenty of time before sunset. A slow day turned into a special afternoon. First, Petska Wetska and then this little girl with stinky shoes."

The marionette prattled on, but Anya fell silent. This was not unusual on their walks. A few minutes passed, and the mountains beyond the forest became visible through the fog. Weeds, bushes, and the shattered remnants of a fallen log littered the winding path up the mountain, but standing against the mountains' edge was a brick tower with a wrought iron gate through which the accordion door to the elevator was visible.

Anya pressed the mother-of-pearl button on the rusted panel, and the gate creaked open. The accordion door folded, revealing the ash panels on the interior of the elevator and another accordion door on the opposite side. A ceiling light flickered as Anya entered the elevator and pressed the button marked with an upward-facing arrow. The door closed, and then the wrought iron gate shut with a thud. The elevator lurched and grumbled as it ascended on the cable. With an echoing bass thud, the elevator came to a stop. The lights flickered, and then the door and gate opened.

An elegant wrought iron fence with an elegant arched gate bordered the Skejik family estate. The family's name and coat of arms, three roses blooming from a single stem, had been sculpted from wrought iron and placed at the top of the gate's arch. Ivy vines climbed the rusting iron spires. Romantically neglected rosebushes with the same twilight sky-colored roses with which Anya decorated the toy shop. Their pollen blended with the fog-moistened air, creating a dreamy haze that perfumed the cool autumnal air. Regardless of weather or season, fog blanketed the Skejik estate grounds.

Anya passed through the gate and walked along the cobblestone path that bifurcated the grounds of the Skejik family home. Shadows rose and fell. Strange forms danced in the distance, their outlines visible at the edge of perception. The the north wind murmured icy whispers as it danced through the air. Anya paid them so little heed, an observer might think she didn't notice them. The dreamy floral scent of these unique roses intensified with each step Anya took.

Halfway along the path, Anya turned left and passed through the gate of the Sejik family cemetery. The gate screeched as she opened it, and even rows of stone crypts where family members were buried stood behind the rows of headstones where the family buried their servants greeted her. Marble and granite statuary filled the empty spaces, their forms veiled by the thick, perfumed fog.

The shades and shadows veiled by the fog dissipated as Anya moved about the cemetery. The whispering wind fell silent. A statue of the Virgin Mary surrounded by children marked the graves of servants' children who died before the age of five. Turning north, Anya made her way to the first row of the above ground crypts. She paused at the newest one, whose marble slab bore only one name and epitaph, *Mikhail Gonshorev, Loyal Friend, Second Father, and Faithful Servant. You will always be missed.*

Placing her hand on slab, Anya said, "I'll see you tomorrow on your birthday, Mikhail, with those salami and tomato sandwiches you loved. Goodbye now. Sleep well."

The family crypts were divided into two sections, one for the Skejik family and one for the in-laws who chose to be buried on the family land. Each generation, a few relatives of those who married into the Skejik family moved into the guest wing of the manor, often an unmarried uncle or aunt or perhaps elderly parents, and when they passed on, they were buried in the family cemetery. Radomir Blinsky, however, chose to rest alongside his wife Katya in the Our Lady of Endless Mercy churchyard.

Anya sat on the granite bench opposite her parents' crypt. Iskra shifted and wrapped her arm around Anya's waist. They sat in a heavy silence for a moment. Through closed eyes, Anya pictured her mother's smiling face and cascading golden curls. Lada Skejik smelled of wood shavings and varnish with floral notes cutting through. Anya smiled. In her mind's eyes, she was six-years-old, sitting on her mother's lap. They were both in Lada's workroom with doll parts strewn on tables around the kiln. They were at the workbench, and Lada guided Anya's tiny hand as she taught her daughter to paint the features on a doll's face.

In the cemetery, tears formed in Anya's eyes, and her smile grew bittersweet. "Those were happy times, Mama. So much more you could have taught me if we had more of the time we had.

I tried to learn all I could, and I tried to keep the traditions you and Dziadzio taught me alive, but I've so many questions for you about things. Mostly, I miss you and Papa." She opened her eyes and saw the drooping wilted flowers in the urn-shaped vase before the crypt. Her cheeks reddened, and Anya lowered her gaze. "I'm sorry, Mama and Papa. I will bring you fresh flowers tomorrow morning. I love you both. Bye now."

Anya and Iskra left the family cemetery and crossed the cobblestone path to the yard of the manor. A smaller cobblestone path passed between the bifurcated garden contained in two massive greenhouses. In a massive greenhouse to the north sat Dr. Boris Skejik's greenhouse filled with medicinal plants and a dozen bushes of the same twilight sky roses and various experimental hybrids the late doctor bred. The family vegetable garden filled the greenhouse to the south of the pass. While Anya no longer performed her father's experiments, she kept the gardens stocked and cared for the plants growing therein.

The Skejik family home began its life as an interpretation of Polish Gothic Revival architecture blended with a Colonial German country townhouse. Shortly before the dawn of the twentieth century, a Victorian town home's tower was added, and when Boris Skejik returned from medical school, he transformed that tower into his office, surgery, and pharmaceutical production lab. The house had been repainted a dozen times to suit the tastes of the family, and the current pale yellow paint had begun to chip, revealing bits of the blue, green, black, gray, and burgundy paints that had adorned the exterior in decades past.

Anya entered the spacious kitchen and set Iskra in the highchair at the table in the breakfast nook, taking care to keep the wires attached to the marionette's appendages from tangling. She then moved through the pantry, the cupboards, and in the white Westinghouse refrigerator, grabbing ingredients to prepare her supper. While milk heated on the stove, Anya chopped and sautéed portobello, cremini, and button mushrooms. When the milk boiled, she added oats, barley, salt, and butter. Once the porridge thickened, she removed it from the heat and folded in the sautéed mushrooms. Anya ladled porridge into a small bowl and then transferred the remainder from the pot into a glass container with a lid.

She placed a spoon in her bowl and then filled a glass with tap water. As she sat at the table, Iskra said, "Oh, mushroom bryjka and water again. You don't want to spice it up with some sausage or maybe some chicken? Or maybe just make a large batch of pierogies. They keep well too."

Anya blew on her food as steam rose from her mushroom porridge. "I do not like that animals are killed for meat, Iskra—not since I saw how the butcher slaughters them. And I like mushrooms in my bryjka. But, I will shop at Bartok's tomorrow and prepare pierogies for the week's meals. With Dożynki a week from tomorrow, we have much work to do."

Iskra nodded. She raised her left hand, turning the palm toward the ceiling, and asked, "What are we going to do, another fairy tale? Maybe something scary for the coming of autumn?"

Anya swallowed the bite she was chewing and then sipped her water. "I had thought about the tale of the Bubak for the first show and then the Wawel Dragon for the second."

Iskra nodded. "Yeah! Parents love when we scare their little brats into behaving. Won't the Wawel dragon be a bit much?"

"It will." Anya nodded. "I've been sketching ideas for how to have the dragon breathe fire while not destroying anything, and I think you would be perfect to be the princess who is rescued by the clever shoemaker."

Iskra blinked, and then her jaw fell limp. She pushed her jaw closed with her hand, and then she said, "Me? Sacrificed and rescued? I've got a better idea. Why don't I play the shoemaker. You can dress me in one of those peasant hoods to hide my face, and then we have a big reveal at the end that the clever shoemaker is a woman, and then she and the princess get married." She leaned closer to Anya. Her eyes twinkled as she asked, "Wouldn't that be more what you want for yourself?"

Anya's face flushed. She choked on her water and then coughed and sputtered. Anya looked away from Iskra, and as she brushed a loose strand of hair beThere's no hind her right ear, she said, "I don't think that's important or a thing or anything, Iskra. The festival is tradition. I can't change the stories."

"Why not? The school library has four different versions of the Wawel Dragon legend from different times in history. You can give them the fifth, and maybe you'll get the attention of a nice girl in the process. Beds are warmer in the winter with two people."

Anya blinked rapidly. She ran her fingers along the length of her spoon and tapped her right foot against the hardwood floor. Her breaths were uneven, quick, and shallow. The redness on her flushed cheeks spread throughout her body. Her hand trembled as she brought the spoon to her lips.

After she swallowed the last spoonful of porridge, Anya said, "I don't think that'll happen. Who would even care that doesn't already know me? Pazat has had no outside blood enter since I turned twenty. You saw it earlier today, Lida isn't the only one who crosses themselves when I'm around."

Anya rose from the table and walked to the sink. As she washed the dishes, Iskra said, "You don't have to be alone."

"I'm not alone. I have you. I have my craft. And I have the books in our library."

Anya set the sponge and pot down in the sink and walked to the kitchen window. A dozen apple trees formed a crescent around a fountain with a giant eagle rising from the center, water spouting from its open beak. She closed her eyes, remembering how her parents would spend every Thursday afternoon sitting among the apple trees with a basket of bread, fruit, and cheese. They talked, laughed, and kissed. Many Thursdays, her father would wrap her mother in his arms and just hold her until the stars shone in the night sky.

She shook her head, shaking the memory from her mind. She offered Iskra a weak smile. "And I have all I need."

Anya walked over and scooped up Iskra. The marionette turned her head and looked up at Anya. Iskra said, "But do you have all you want?"

A heavy sigh fell from Anya's lips. "It is too much to even ask of another, especially with the curse."

Iskra closed her eyes. "If the curse is real and not some rumor those damned Sullivans started to justify their daughter's harassment of you when you were children. Really? *Her father's wanton and unholy experiments left her unable to remain outside the family grounds beyond the stroke of midnight, or she will surely wither like a rose without water.* How is a curse like that believable in this day and age?"

Anya closed her eyes. "Better to remain safe and not test it. Things will remain as they are."

While Anya dined alone in her manor high in the mountains above Pazat, the local diner, Karrolton's Café, teemed with residents who walked through the dense fog to gather as they prepared for Dożynki, the annual harvest festival. While the festival normally coincides with the Feast of the Assumption of Mary, the rains that pelted the town over the last two weeks necessitated pushing the festival back to the end of August.

Now, as the day of the celebration neared, a lively crowed filled the dozen booths with their green leather upholstery. Two waitresses, both looked to be in their late teens, ran food and drink from the kitchen to the diners. Most of the adults indulged in a pint of beer from the town's brewery, Beerogi Brewing, or a glass of wine from the local winery, Sullivan Vineyards. As a result, lively chatter, laughter, and the occasional angry word filled the air.

Of course, gossip consumed several discussions. Much of it was standard small town gossip. Infidelity, arguments, and a pig theft were the talks of the day, as expected; however, there was one other hot topic of discussion at a few tables. Who was this new resident scheduled to move into Danforth Alexander's home next week?

"I heard it was his eldest son's granddaughter. You know, the son who ran away after that hippie Lutheran girl from Hawley he met at college", one brunette with cat's eye spectacles said, turning to the man behind her.

"Yeah? Not what I heard," the man replied. His bushy blond mustache swayed "Father Slivkin said he heard from someone in the line waiting for confession that the girl is from Danforth's daughter's line."

"That can't be," one of the waitresses, a plus-sized redhead with gray eyes, chimed in as she brought the man another beer and an order of pierogies. "Mister Alexander's lawyer was in here earlier, and he said the girl's last name was Alexander. So, it has to be one of the sons' families, right?"

An older man who wore a fishing cap to cover his wild, scraggly gray hair butted into the conversation. "Well, she must be a good Catholic girl, at least. I heard she's attending St. Albertus Magnus in Nouvelle Arniers. I don't know the school, but it's named for a saint, and it's in Louisiana, a Catholic state. So, she'll fit in just fine."

"As long as she's not from the younger son's line," the first woman said. "I remember when he was a teenager. You never saw a lazier, more disrespectful disgrace of a person."

An old man with sun-leathered skin leaned over and twirled his handlebar mustache. "People are like crops and cattle. If there's something in them you don't like, you got to breed it out of them. Couple of generations go by, and things can be mighty different."

"Ain't nothing saintly about that Nouvelle Arniers," another man said from two tables over. He was a heavyset man in his mid-forties with a receding salt and pepper hairline. "That's one wicked city if ever I saw one, and that school, it's named after an alchemist. We don't need another one of those in town."

"So," the redhead waitress asked. "Vassar College was named for a brewer, and they don't teach brewing there. Besides, no one studies alchemy at universities. They teach chemistry."

As the conversation continued, the diner's door burst open, momentarily silencing all conversations. A tall, conventionally active woman with curly blonde hair, blue eyes, and fair skin strode through the door wearing a red dress with a black belt and black riding boots. Everyone greeted her, and she returned their greetings with grandiose smiles and pageant hand waves. Lida Petska waved her hand frantically. She shouted, "Carolyn! I saved you a seat."

Carolyn walked over and sat down. Within seconds both waitresses were at the table, one taking Carolyn's order and the other bringing her a glass of her favorite wine, a basket of fresh bread, and a slice of carrot cake. Carolyn smiled and nodded.

"Good job, Lida," Carolyn said. "A seat in the corner. You were always a corner-sitter, weren't you?"

She laughed. Lida looked at her plate, pushing the mashed potatoes to the side. "You don't have to remind me."

Carolyn sipped the wine. "Well? Did you do what I asked this time?"

Lida nodded emphatically. "I did. Anya said the doll will be ready by Friday. I'll go pick it up then."

"And pay for it."

Lida choked on the soda she was sipping. Carolyn laughed as Lida scrambled to wipe herself. "But her dolls are expensive. I thought you just wanted me to set things up."

Carolyn gagged and rolled her eyes. "I want nothing to do with that freak and her little dolls. I certainly won't give her any of my money. That's where you come in. You don't want my sweet little Elisa to be sad, do you?"

Lida shook her head. "No, no I don't. Okay. Why do you hate her so much anyway? She doesn't bother anyone, just does her own thing."

Carolyn scrunched her face into a scowl. She stabbed her pork chop with the fork and then sliced it with uneven, jagged strokes. "Why do I need a reason to hate that repulsive freak who won't talk to anyone without that doll? She even throws her voice when it's not in her hands. And how has she kept that charade up since we were children? It's not right. She should be locked away and wearing a straitjacket."

Lida shoved an oversized spoonful of mashed potatoes into her mouth while Carolyn spoke. With her mouth full, she said, "But it's not like she was always like that. The doll didn't show up until after you burned her face with those chemicals we stole from the science closet—"

"You stole," Carolyn said. "You stole those chemicals, Lida And why do you care? So, she was pretty with her black hair and soft hands and the way she smiled like a dumb puppy when she did anything around us. It was weird. She's not natural. She's not one of us. You know that."

Lida tilted her head and scrunched her face. She shook her head. "But, Carolyn, her family has been in Pazat since it was founded—both sides of her family. Your parents moved here right before you started school. Sure, her family is Polish while most of us are either Czech or Ukrainian, but she's a Slav."

Carolyn crossed herself and then glared. A low growl rumbled through her tense, tight lips. "I shouldn't have to spell it out for you." A smile burst across Carolyn's face as she turned toward an elderly priest who approached their table. "Oh, hello, Father Slivkin. It's so good to see you."

Father Slivkin, an older man with a bald head and a bushy gray beard, approached the table and said, "Hello, Carolyn. We're so happy Danika will be this year's Dożynki maiden, and we greatly appreciate your generous donation to help acquire new stained-glass windows."

Carolyn beamed with a sly smile. "It was my pleasure, Father. I love God with every fiber of my being, and as a mother myself, I couldn't bear to let the images of our Savior's blessed and holy mother fall into disrepair. She is such an inspiration. If there is any leftover, Father, please donate it to a food bank."

The old priest nodded. "Of course. Thank you again. I look forward to seeing in mass on Sunday."

"I would never dream of missing it."

The waitress brought Carolyn her meal. After she had finished dining, she ate the carrot cake in front of Lida and then excused herself, thanking Lida for supper. When the waitress handed Lida the ticket, she asked the older woman, "Miss Petska, why do you let her do that to you?"

"What do you mean?"

"You know, boss you around and just be mean to you. The young waitress shrugged her shoulders. "I know it's not my place to tell my elders what to do, but you don't seem too happy about it. That's all."

Lida waved the young woman's words away. "It's not like that at all. Carolyn's really nice, once you get to know her. We've been friends since school. This is just the way she is."

The waitress nodded. "Well, seems like if that's the way she is, maybe you need to outgrow her. I don't wear the clothes I wore in kindergarten. Sometimes friends are like that. It sucks, but it do be like that sometimes."

After paying for her meal and for Carolyn's meal, Lida Petska left as generous a tip as she could afford and went home.

3

Thursday morning, Sara completed her run early so she could run one final errand before Andrea Jones-Cook arrived at noon to help with moving. She drove to her favorite locally owned bookstore and café, The Ink and Quill. When the new owners, Harold and Rhianna Stephens bought the building, which had the distinction of being the oldest bar in the state, the city recoiled in horror at the mention of their desire to turn a beloved watering hole into a bookstore. Sara smiled, remembering laughing and mocking the protesters from her apartment as she followed what the local newspaper, The Daily Arniersian, dubbed "The Scandal of the Decade". Of course, once the shop and café opened, the traditional pub aesthetics, the amazing food (and quality beer and wine served on weekends), the quality service, and the increased number of permanent jobs that the Stephenses brought to the town persuaded the locals to embrace this new development—at least on the weekends.

Fortunately for bibliophiles, the Stephenses thought ahead and had a soundproof wall built to separate the bookstore from the café, allowing shoppers to browse the rich maple shelves in peace. Strategically placed electric wax melting pots perfumed the bookstore with the welcoming autumnal scent of baked apples spiced with cinnamon, coriander, ginger, and clove. Sara waved to the young woman working the register, a former student of hers, and sauntered over to the gifts section to select four leather sketchbooks, two black, one lavender, and one burgundy.

As she looked over the charcoal pencils and colored ink pens in the bookstore's ever-growing art supply section, a friendly voice broke her silence, saying, "So, which class is lucky enough to get hand-drawn study guides this semester?"

Sara beamed as she turned toward the voice. "Hi, Nadi. How's school going?"

The young woman shrugged. "School's school. I was hoping to have you for 2501 this semester, but I guess your section filled up too fast."

Nadia Kobos was in her early twenties. A volleyball player for the St. Albertus Magnus Screaming Fiends, she was a svelte woman with olive skin, lustrous black hair pulled into a ponytail, and chestnut brown eyes. "So, is the meme right?"

"The meme?" Sara raised an eyebrow and tilted her head. She grabbed a massive box of colored pencils, a large vinyl packet of black ink pens of various thicknesses, and an assortment of colored inks.

"You know, the one about never asking a grad student about their dissertation."

Sara snorted and narrowed her eyes. Darkness shadowed her face for a second. As she clenched her jaw, her lips narrowed and disappeared. Her muscles tensed. Sara blinked, and her smile returned. She shrugged. "I've just got one edit—a bit one, but only one—in the fourth chapter, which means one chapter remains. I should graduate in May."

Nadia giggled. She asked, "Great! Anyway, need any help finding stuff?"

"I don't know, Nadi," Sara said, adding the book to her stack. "I've got a few sketchbooks and art supplies, which I hope will last me the rest of the semester. I'm good there, but if you could help me find something to read, something light and distracting, I'll make sure you get the commission for my sale."

Nadia scratched behind her ear. "I see you in here all the time, but I don't recall you ever buying a book that wasn't a sketchbook. Not that your art isn't awesome. I mean, who doesn't love having hand-drawn portraits of historical figures on their study guides? Made your class so cool. Oh, anyway, what do you normally read?"

Sara shifted the massive stack of art supplies from one arm to the other. "Nothing too out there. Historical fiction, mostly. Mysteries sometimes. I'm caught up on my favorites, Destiny Grimm, Ellery Adams, Laura Childs, Fiona Grace, Penny Brooke, and Nancy Warren. I like books I can curl up with under a blanket with a cup of tea and have a good read. It's just…"

Her voice trailed off into a forlorn silence as she scanned the shelves. A handful of shoppers browsed the Magazines, True Crime, Science Fiction, Local Cookbooks, and History sections. Most were middle-aged, and half had small children with them. Sara shook her head. Her shoulders slumped. "I guess I've found everything."

"No, it's that you want something new." Nadia thought for a moment and then flashed a mischievous smile. "Do you trust me?"

Sara squinted and scrunched her face. She shrugged. "Yeah. Why?"

"Then close your eyes and follow me. We're going on a pilgrimage to find you a new storyteller."

Sara closed her eyes and shook her head. Nadia grabbed Sara's hand and led her through the rows of shelves. After half a dozen turns, they reached the carefully selected shelf. Nadia directed her former teacher to open her eyes. Sara opened her eyes and surveyed the shelf before her.

"Really?" She exclaimed in shock. "I ask for a recommendation, and you bring me to the *Romance* section?"

"You said you wanted something different, something new, something you're not getting." Sara glared at Nadia. Nadia waved a dismissive hand. "Tell me I'm wrong. Also, you're a great teacher, and you're super friendly and always vibing with the people around you. But I've never seen you bring a date here, and trust me, a *lot* of women use a bookstore date as a way to test a partner. Point is, you could use a happy ending. So, here we are."

"But, Nadia, look at these titles. *A Hard Man to Love. The Duke's Woman. Sweet, Savage Love.*" Sara read the titles in a mocking breathless voice. "You can't expect me to read these."

"Someone didn't understand the assignment," Sara said. "Why don't you look at the shelf I actually placed you in front of? They're new, and Miss Rhianna faced some backlash from Boomers when she set up the shelf."

Sara rolled her eyes and turned back to the shelf. Exploring the titles on the brightly colored spines as her index finger glided gently from book to book, she slowly began to understand Nadia's purpose. "These are—these are *lesbian* romance novels," she whispered.

"You don't have to whisper it, Miss Sara, and if the pride flag you had in your office when I took your class and the Tumblr feed I glanced at when you left your laptop open while I refilled your coffee cup last week are any indication, you have an interest in this." She smiled triumphantly.

Sara brushed her hair behind her left ear and shifted like a teenager whose parents caught them sneaking into the house hours after curfew. "It's just fan art and fanfiction, and I—well—I," She sighed and continued in hushed tones. "Alright, Nadi, yes, you're right." Then she hastily added, "But I've never bought any."

Nadia Kobos stretched out her hand and plucked one book from the shelf and placed it on top of Sara's stack. She smiled. "Think of it as life advice—free therapy that I learned during my own sessions. If you want something new, you have to break you out of your safe and comfy comfort zone once in a while. Until you work up the courage to do that for real, you can at least live vicariously through the romantic adventure, penned by L. E. Stapleton, *Caught in the Weaver's Dark Web*."

Sara rolled her eyes as she flipped to the back cover and skimmed the book's summary. *Violet Summers had just moved to Görenburg to escape her family. Donna Battenbon spends all of her time weaving blankets and sewing clothing in the shop she inherited from her family. When the two meet at the Festival of the First Planting, their chemistry is undeniable. As the fires of passion build, will Violet's fears and Donna's secrets smother the flames?*

Sara stared blankly at Nadia. "This is just as cheesy as the other books here."

"Perhaps," Nadia conceded. "But you wanted something different, and you stated that you trust my recommendations. We were each randomly assigned to read five books in this section so we could help customers, this was one of mine. I'm not into girls—at least I don't think so—but even I found it hot."

Sara laughed. "Alright. I'll give it a shot. I could use a distraction right now."

"Books are friends that are always there for you," Nadia said, smiling. "You popping over to the café for lunch like usual?"

Sara shook her head. "I wish, I'm packing up for a move. Long story, I'd rather not go into it, but thank you."

Nadia nodded. The two women chatted as they walked to the register. Sara paid for her books and left the store. She stopped by Sicilian Pie and grabbed two margherita pizzas and then drove home.

With the cardboard pizza boxes open on the kitchen table, Sara arranged her charcoal pencils, the black ink pens, and the colored pencils around the top of the lavender sketchbook. With one hand holding the book *Caught in the Weaver's Dark Web* open and the other holding a pencil, Sara prepared to sketch any characters and scenes from the book that caught her interest.

Three chapters in, a fire ravaged sweet Violet Summers' house in the small town, but Donna Battenbon offered to let her rent a wing of the her family manor until her home was fixed. During that time, Violet fell in love with the massive collection of ancient books in the Battenbon family library. As Sara's mind drifted to her own search for an ancient book, the doorbell sounded.

Sara opened the door, and her jaw dropped. Andrea stood on the doorstep along with Elisabeth St. Clair and Barbara Goldberg. Andrea's ponytail peeked over the shoulder of her burgundy turtleneck. Elisabeth had just dyed her ringlets pink, purple, and blue. She wore an oversized purple and black plaid flannel shirt with her lacy burgundy bra strap and the olive skin of her right shoulder showing. Barbara's gold Magen David stud earrings sparkled in the sunlight with her thick brown hair pulled in a loose bun.

"The Sara Alexander Moving Committee has arrived," Andrea said with her arms open.

"You," Sara said through a massive grin. "All of you? You came to help?"

Elisabeth raised the two large canvas bags she carried over her head. She pushed her way into the townhouse and handed Sara the bags. "And we brought snacks for today and for you on your trip."

Barbara crossed her arms over her chest and spoke in a matter-of-fact voice. "First order of business. I have seen no moving truck, so your hired movers are not here. Where are your sex toys?"

Sara laughed. "Packed in the Civic. I hope she makes the trip. The movers will be here in an hour. They're supposed to box things up if needed, load the truck, and then drive to Pazat and unload."

"So, what's left to do," Andrea asked.

Sara ran her fingers through her hair as she exhaled. Shaking her head, she said, "Just box books, knick knacks, and video games up, I guess. I've got everything else done. The only furniture of mine I'm taking is in my bedroom. Oh! And there are two margherita pizzas."

"Then let's get started!" Elisabeth raced toward the stairs.

Working together, the four women had everything packed by the time the movers arrived. Within an hour, the three men Sara's mother hired had all of Sara's possessions loaded into their truck. Once the truck was loaded, the lead driver approached Sara to confirm the destination, explain the route they planned to take, and provide an estimated arrival time. Sara confirmed she would be there earlier, as she had to meet her late great grandfather's attorney to get the keys. They shook hands, and the movers started on their journey.

A massive smile broadened her face as Sara hugged her friends. "I'm going to miss you all. Please, keep me informed on departmental gossip. And Elisabeth, I expect you to blow up my texts if Drew and Wade kiss."

"Oh you know I will." Elisabeth said. "And we're all just a Zoom call away."

Barbara nodded. "And we can still do Pajama Happy Hour."

"And I'll come see you over Fall break, if not before."

Sara nodded. "I look forward to it."

"And text us when you stop for the night. Oh, and when you get there," Barbara said.

"And give us a video tour of your new house!" Elisabeth said.

"And this town too. I can't find anything about it other than a dot on a map and a connection to Poland and Ukraine."

"I will. Thank you. All of you." Goodbyes continued for another half hour before Sara drove her Civic off to the northeast.

Sara Alexander passed through Honesdale, Pennsylvania, at two o'clock in the afternoon on Saturday. Her Friday was spent driving, starting before dawn and checking into a roadside motel just before sunset when she entered Wayne County. This allowed her to sleep in before the final leg of her journey, and the highway traffic flowed in her favor.

As she exited the highway, Sara filled her fuel tank at the first Exxon gas station she came. She paid for gas and then braved the filthy, malodorous restroom with a perpetually leaking sink. Back in her blue Civic, Sara opened a small bag of trail mix and raised it to her mouth, eating directly from the bag. She slurped the last drops of her Dunkin Donuts iced coffee as she returned to the road.

Siri directed her onto an uneven, cracked, pothole-riddled two lane road, and then her mom called. Sara rolled her eyes and sent the call to the speakers. "Hi, Mom. What do you need?"

"There you are, Sara." Frantic exasperation saturated her mother's voice. "Where are you? I called Denis Novák, granddad's attorney and estate executor, and he said you weren't there yet. I thought you might have turned around and gone back to that sinful Catholic city."

"I thought about it, Mom," Sara said. "But since the movers have most of my stuff, it would be a bad decision. I'd have my clothes, my laptop, my dolls, and my sex toys."

"Sara Daphne Alexander, I do not need to hear such talk. You'll need to get rid of those if you hope to find yourself a husband acceptable by your great grandfather's standards."

Sara crunched on a handful of seasoned hard pretzel sticks. With her mouth full, she said, "About that, Mom. I'm going to ask him if it has to be a husband. Maybe the wording was just spouse."

Her mother sighed. "Don't talk with your mouth full. No man wants that in a wife. And no, the stipulation in his will, Sara Daphne Alexander, is that you live in his house until you meet a good man and get married. It has to be a husband. We're a Christian family, and we believe marriage is between one man and one woman. Maybe this will get you out of that little phase of yours before you die in your sin."

"It's not a phase, Mom." Sara's voice lowered a full octave, and she growled her words as she spoke. "And before you bring in the money thing again, I know that I screw over the entire family if I don't do this."

"Don't think of it that way, Sara. That city you wetre in is a wicked city. Did you know they've legalized prostitution, abortion, *and* homosexual marriage?"

Sara smirked. "That last one is one reason I chose this school."

"I don't want to hear about that, young lady. You know that's not how we raised you. An abomination is what that is. Think of what an opportunity you have to get away from that trashy apartment you live in, get a better car than that twelve-year-old foreign thing, and get your heart right with Jesus."

"I've worked hard for that car," Sara said. And she had. She came from old money, but Sara Alexander had worked throughout college, saved her money, and paid for that blue Honda Civic when she finished her undergraduate studies. That car saw her through four moves, seven girlfriends, and five job changes during her graduate education in Nouvelle Arniers, Louisiana.

"Of course you have, dear," her mother said. "No one denies that, but you can't live like that forever. This will give you a chance to gain the security we've given you that allowed you to pursue your little degree. No man will want—"

"But a woman will, Mom." Sara switched on the headlights. "Shit! Where'd this fog come from? Look, Mom, I'm going to let you go. I need to focus on the road. Call you when I get there. Love you. Bye."

The fog obscured her vision beyond fifteen feet. Sara slowed her speed. Half an hour passed, and the fog thinned enough for Sara to see the shapes of fences and fields on both sides of her. A shiver ran through her spine. She exhaled a sigh of relief as she saw a broken wooden sign welcoming her to Pazat.

"So, this is it? A foggy little farm town. Maybe it's cute when the sun's out."

Sara eyed the town as she listened to Siri's directions. *There are a lot of vintage trucks here*, she thought. *The creepy fog aside, the town's kind of cute, and these cobblestone streets remind me of the Old Quarter of Nouvelle Arniers. It's not French, but it's like Russian? No! Romanian? Maybe, but it's like something from Eastern Europe.*

Following the verbal directions from her GPS, she made her way to the town square. Giant wreaths made from wheat and flowers, tied with bright red and gold ribbons, adorned the doors on all the buildings and the lamp posts. Three residents paused to watch her car as it drove through the town's streets. *It's got a town square! That's so cool, and it looks like they decorated it for some festival. Wonder what it was. Did I miss it? That would be a fun way to meet the neighbors. I'll ask Mr. Novák. Oh! I almost forgot. Let me call him now.*

She alerted her great grandfather's attorney she had arrived in Pazat. A few more turns brought her to the house. A long, slow whistle slid from her lips as she gazed upon the two-story Tudor Revival home whose second story overhung the first, creating a covered porch. An arched door resembling the multi-paned windows opened to a parapet-framed balcony. She parked her car on the side of the driveway, leaving the area closest to the front door for the movers.

Sara knocked on the door, expecting no one to answer, and she was not disappointed. A few moments passed before a silver Chevrolet Impala parked beside her. A slender, elderly man with two tufts of white hair sticking out from above his ears exited the car. Thick black-framed spectacles perched on the bridge of his nose, and he wore a three-piece, charcoal suit and carried a brown leather attaché case.

After he ascended the stairs to the covered porch, he shook Sara's hand and said, "Ah, Miss Alexander, it's a pleasure to meet you, if under these unfortunate circumstances. I'm Denis Novák, and I was Danforth's attorney and the executor of his last will and testament."

His voice was a nasal baritone. Sara nodded. "Thank you. This wasn't exactly how I expected to start the fifth year of my doctoral program, but life's an adventure."

He nodded. "I'm sorry you had to put your education on hold, but yes, life is an adventure."

"I'm not putting it on hold. I just need to figure out who'll provide Wi-Fi."

"I hope you won't need much," he said in an apologetic tone. "Cellular phones and Internet services tend to be spotty at times here. It's a combination of the mountains and the moisture in the air, I suppose. It frustrates the younger generations, but they acclimate. Do you need help with your possessions?"

"Thank you." Sara shook her head. "But a moving company will be here on Monday with everything I couldn't fit in my car, and I can empty my car as long as I have daylight."

"Good." He produced an iron key from his blazer's inner breast pocket and unlocked the door. He opened it and gestured for Sara to enter, saying, "After you. We just have a few things to take care of."

He followed Sara into the foyer, flipping on the overhead light. A faint smell of burnt wood caught Sara's nose. The house was impeccably clean, and Sara voiced a whispered *wow* at the gorgeous hardwood floors, silver-framed mirrors, and porcelain vases filled with fresh flowers. Denis Novák placed his attaché case on one of the marble-topped tables against the wall on Sara's left.

Mr. Novák frowned. "I pleaded with Mr. Alexander to approve electricians to inspect the wiring, but it seems he never did. I offer the same advice to you."

"Yes, sir. It's cleaner than I expected," Sara said. "But he did only die last week."

"That, and using Mister Alexander's funds, I hired cleaners to make the house presentable. His clothing has been laundered and placed in boxes as well. We just have a few papers to sign. The first states you have taken possession of the house and agree to complete the terms set forth in his will. The other three grant me permission to transfer the electricity, telephone, and homeowner insurance services to your name, thus avoiding any lapse in service."

Sara sighed. Her smile cracked for a brief second. "Does the will actually state I have to marry an acceptable man, or was that my mom being herself?"

He chuckled. "Yes, I admit it is an antiquated request, but it is legal. And yes, he also provided a list of characteristics this man must have. Will that be a problem?"

"Aside from the fact that you can't force love, there's the whole part about me being a lesbian."

Denis Novák frowned. "Yes, that does complicate matters, but you have three years to make the best decision for you and your family. Yes? I will had you the keys to the house. If there is anything else you need, my card is included with your paperwork. You may retain my services at my standard rate. You will find the one hundred thousand dollar monthly allowance granted you is more than sufficient for your expenses and my services. Welcome to Pazat."

"I think having an attorney would be wise, given the complexities of all of this."

"Then I shall draw up the contract on Monday, but you are now my client, Miss Alexander."

They shook hands once more, and the attorney departed. Sara texted her friends to let them know she had arrived and then set about unloading her car. Elegant antique furnishings filled the house. Sara noted she would only need to purchase a new television for the great room, some new rugs, and LED bulbs for all the lamps. Upon inspecting the kitchen, she sighed. The pantry and refrigerator were empty.

"Well," she said, grabbing the backpack she used instead of a casual purse. "I hope there's a diner or an open grocery store in this town."

As she exited the front door, two women stepped from a Land Rover carrying aluminum foil-covered dishes. One was a tall blonde, conventionally attractive, with curly hair, blue eyes, and fair skin. She wore a burgundy dress with ruffled cuffs and a high collar as well as a pair of black boots. The other was Lida Petska. The blonde had a broad smile on her face, but Lida appeared nervous.

Sara returned the blonde woman's smile. "Hi, I'm Sara. I guess you figured I just moved in."

"We heard a few rumors around town that you arrived today," the blonde woman said. "And hello, Sara, was it? Yes, good. I'm Carolyn Ward. You passed my farm on the way in. It's the larger of the two farms right at the edge of town. And this is my good friend Lida Petska."

Carolyn elbowed Lida, who said, "Oh, hi. Welcome to Pazat."

"It's a pleasure to meet you," Sara said. "I'd invite you inside, but the pantry's empty."

Carolyn sighed and offered sympathy. "We are so sorry for your family's loss, and well, the cleaners who prepared the house probably took everything. Some people are like that."

"At least it went to people who could use it. Better than anything going to waste."

"Yes," Carolyn said. "Well, we wanted to welcome you and ease your first night or two. We brought you three dozen pierogies and a cheesecake topped with fresh apple compote. Everything is disposable, so you don't have to worry about returning anything."

"Thank—thank you." Sara accepted the covered plates and stacked them on a side table just inside the front door. "I really do appreciate this. It's been a long drive, and I wasn't looking forward to grocery shopping today. Guess I'll go tomorrow."

Carolyn frowned. She shook her head. "You're not from here, so you wouldn't know. All businesses close on Sundays, especially tomorrow for Dożynki. Will you join us at the festival?"

Sara tilted her head to the right and lifted her left eyebrow. "Dożynki? What's that?"

Carolyn smiled. "It's our harvest festival, and it celebrates the Assumption of Mary. It's a week late this year due to weather and crop cycles, but it means you can join us. My daughter Danika has been chosen as the year's Dożynki maiden. She will lead the procession from the edge of our farm to our church in the square. There will be food, games, and a traditional dance. It would be a great way to meet your neighbors. I hope you'll join us."

Sara nodded vigorously. "I'd love to. I saw the decorations as I passed the square on my way in. Do I just show up at the square?"

Carolyn nodded. "Around two in the afternoon. We'd also love if you joined us for church in the morning. Everyone will be there." She smirked and then added, "Well, all the good people you should meet."

Sara looked around. "This seems like a quiet little town. Are there bad people?"

Lida shook her head. "No, there's no one who's a bad person or anyth—Ugh!"

Carolyn ground her heel into the top of Lida's foot, maintaining a smile. She blushed. "No one is bad, per se, but there is one person who never attends. But she was raised by heretics, so I suppose we shouldn't expect more of her."

"Oh, well, that's good to know. Thank you." Sara smiled. *Small towns are all alike, and I have to be here for three years.* "Well, I'm going to enjoy this food and get some sleep. I'll see you tomorrow at the festival for sure.

The thin veil of fog sparkled as the sun's warming, welcoming light. Sara slipped into a sports bra and athletic leggings. She then ate two of the pierogies and a cup of cold brewed ice coffee for breakfast. After putting her earbuds into her ear and starting her *Morning Run* playlist, which was a blend of pop, pop punk, and upbeat baroque music, she locked the door behind her and headed out for her morning run.

The air was cool, and crisp. The sweet smell of freshly cut hay blended with the earthiness of fresh grains. As she jogged away from the mountains, the fresh smells of apples being picked and juiced cut through the fresh earthiness of the fields. The occasional dog followed her along her run until the fences halted the dogs' progress. She saw no people, but she surmised they were attending mass in the one church she saw on her way in.

She jogged to the town square, which had been further decorated and dressed for the Dożynki festival. Booths for food and crafts, all adorned with flower and grain wreaths, were set up but unattended. Light from within Our Lady of Endless Mercy illuminated the scenes of martyred saints and the life of Christ depicted on the stained glass windows. She turned to the north east around the side of the church and slammed into an old woman setting up what appeared to be a fortune teller's booth.

"I'm so sorry," Sara said as she regained her balance. "I didn't expect anyone would be out this early. Let me help you."

Sara kneeled on the cobblestone, picking up the box the old woman dropped. Heavy wrinkles creased the leathery olive skin of the woman's face, but her eyes sparkled and danced like those of someone half the age Sara assumed her to be. She wrapped her hair in a purple scarf with embroidered red and gold flowers and wore a brown cardigan over a maxi dress with a white bodice and purple skirt adorned with red flowers at the hem. Gold jewelry, adorned with jingling bells, hung from her neck and wrists.

She took the box from Sara and smiled, her eyes searching Sara's face. "Thank you, child. Oh, you're the Alexander heir." She laughed. "The wind carried you in time for the Dożynki. Welcome, welcome. You're early, but why not start the day with knowledge? Step into my parlor."

The old woman gestured to the small tented booth of midnight purple adorned with golden corn, wheat, and flowers. Sara shrugged and nodded. "Sure."

The old woman hobbled into her tent and moved to the chair behind the table at its center. Four large wooden chicken feet protruded from the central column supporting it. With a quick gesture, the old woman lit the four tall black pillar candles near the table's center. As Sara sat at the chair opposite the woman, the old woman produced a deck of cards and began shuffling.

"I don't mean to distract you," Sara said. "But I've been rude, and I'm sorry. My name's Sara. And I don't have cash on me, since I'm just out for a run."

The old woman switched to a Faro shuffle and smirked. "Money is not required here, and you may call me Baba. Everyone needs a grandmother, no?"

Sara nodded rapidly. "I love my grandmother. Well, I loved both of them, but my mom's mom died when I was five. My dad's mom always encouraged me to be myself, to love what I loved, and to take risks. I wouldn't be who I am without her."

Baba smiled and pushed the deck toward Sara. "Three cards, as a busy day lies before you. Cut the cards and pass them back."

Sara cut the cards and passed them back to Baba. The old woman nodded. With the middle and ring fingers of her right hand, Baba slid three cards from the top of the deck and placed them in a line between the two women. She flipped over the first card and said, "The Eight of Cups inverted, a moment of unhappy, unsuccessful, or undesired transition. Perhaps avoiding an argument with someone to avoid trouble. Now, don't say anything, Sara dear. Let's see what's next for more inspiration."

She flipped the second card, another inverted card. "A maternal figure, when inverted, the Pentacle Queen smothers with her jealousy and self-centeredness. Seems a mother who desires what she wants for your life is someone with whom you need to have a real conversation, but you've avoided it. I hope you didn't run away to Pazat to avoid her."

Baba chuckled. Her eyes never broke their contact with Sara's eyes. The younger woman swallowed hard and pulled at the strap of her sports bra. Her voice cracked as she said, "I—well—I tried to have the conversation, but she... What's the final card say?"

Baba's yellowed, uneven teeth became visible in her toothy smile. She nodded and flipped the final card. She raised her right eyebrow. "Ah, here's a bit of sunlight for you, dearie. If you show Strength, compassion, gentleness, and courage, the lion threatening to devour you will be tamed. Now, nothing is written in the stones of the earth, so take this as advice and enjoy your time in Pazat."

Sara nodded and smiled. "Thank you, Baba. I hope to see you around."

Sara rose and backed out of the tent, and then awkwardly returned to her run. Baba nodded and smiled. She slid the next card from the top of the deck. A nude woman holding a wand in each hand danced amidst a wreath of flowers. Baba said, "If your strength is of the proper kind, then the World will be yours with all of the harmony, fulfillment, and sense of belonging that goes along with it. You will be who you are in the place where who you are is needed, wanted, and desired."

After a long, hot shower, Sara did her makeup quickly and then spent the next three hours choosing an outfit for her first harvest festival in Pazat. She wanted to make the right impression, and from previous interactions, she assumed religious people populated the town. Plus, the weather was cool, and too much exposed skin would make her cold. She laughed. Five years of living in Louisiana, and she had forgotten how to handle a northern fall. Louisiana summers were still brutal. Eventually, she settled on a burgundy turtleneck, gray and black plaid skirt, burgundy tights, and a pair of black Doc Marten Mary Janes. Grabbing her mini backpack, she headed out the door and walked to the town square.

Pazat's residents packed the town square by the time Sara arrived, forming two lines on its north and south sides. Many of them wore what Sara assumed to be some sort of traditional garb. Children laughed, played with little wooden toys, and danced. Adults ate various street foods, chatted with each other about various topics, and attempted—sometimes successfully—to corral their children. Teenagers played on their phones, ignoring everyone around them. A large black carriage pulled by wooden horses drew her attention. *Must be a replica of something from the old days.*

Conversations halted as Sara milled about the crowd. Eyes stared at her before whispers of *Oh, that's the Alexander girl, She's too young to be on her own*, and *She's older than I thought she would be* echoed in Sara's ears. She smiled and waved. She passed the northern side of the church, but she didn't see Baba's little tent. She shrugged. Maybe it moved.

Sara joined the crowd as they started cheering. She didn't know what was happening, but everyone seemed happy. After a few minutes, their cheering reached a crescendo as a throng of teenage girls in white chemises with pink, yellow, and blue flowers around the neck and hem.

The leader of the procession, a conventionally attractive girl with a bob of blonde sausage curls and sea foam green eyes, wore a crown of flowers and held aloft a tall pole with a crossbar near the top over which a massive wreath similar to those on the doors of buildings was hung. The woman Sara met yesterday, Carolyn Ward, pushed her way to the front of the crowd, her cell phone held high as she recorded the throng's entry into the square.

The girls skipped as they moved, giggling and gasping as their bare feet touched the cold cobblestones of the town square. The town's priest, an older man with no hair save for a bushy silver beard, exited the church through the arched double doors. He extended his hands, palms forward, as the girls reached the church. They stopped and dropped to their knees. Everyone crossed themselves and fell silent. The lead girl lowered the pole. The priest took the wreath, prayed over it and the harvest, and placed the wreath on the church door. The crowd cheered again and then dispersed to enjoy the rest of the festival.

Sara walked around the food stalls, purchasing a trio of pierogies, a skewer of seasoned corn on the cob, and a half dozen fried cheese sticks. There weren't many vegetarian options. As she perused a local glassblower's wares, a man about her father's age and size greeted her, saying, "You must be Danforth's great-granddaughter. I'm Drago Mozoroff, the town's mayor. I'm sorry for your loss, but I want to welcome you and hope you're settling in well, all things considered."

Sara met his genuine smile with one of her own. She nodded. "I'm Sara. Things are going well. I've met a few people. This festival seems like a fun time. Just hoping I can get some groceries tomorrow and get some level of Wi-Fi access set up, since my great grandfather didn't use the 'net. Then I'll be peachy."

Mayor Mozoroff nodded. "Good to hear. Good to hear. If you haven't heard, we have spotty cellular and wireless reception here. No one's sure why. You'll get used to things closing on Sundays, and tomorrow, Karelewski's will be open. Well, enjoy your day. It's a pleasure to have you here. Let me know if you need anything as you settle in."

He excused himself and walked away. Sara had half a dozen more conversations like that with other residents. Sara's smile broadened. The place looked weird, but the people were friendly. Maybe this wouldn't be so bad after all.

As she walked around the northern edge of the square, she saw all the younger children, a handful of teenagers, and that woman Lida Petska sat on benches before a small stage where marionettes performed a play. The banner atop the stage read *Skejik Marionette Theatre*. The marionettes were beautiful, lifelike and expressive in their crafting. Though Sara saw the strings, the marionettes appeared to have more moving parts than two hands could control. There had to be two puppeteers. As Sara joined the audience, a messenger marionette delivered the message from King Krak that he would offer a room filled with gold and the hand of his daughter in marriage to any who could slay the dragon terrorizing the town. Another marionette wearing a medieval peasant's hooded cowl that covered the face, claimed to be a shoemaker and then promised to slay the dragon. The shoemaker killed a sheep and stuffed it with sulfur.

Carrying it to the dragon's cave, the shoemaker dropped the sheep at the entrance and then hid behind a rock. The dragon, a frightful creature with shimmering metallic scales and smoke curling from its nostrils, leaped out and devoured the sheep whole. The dragon screamed as the sulfur burned its stomach, and as it flew off to get water, it exploded in a ball of fire. Wooden body parts flew into the crowd. Children cheered and laughed.

The shoemaker then approached the princess. The princess' voice was soft but trembled anxiously as she said, "Thank you, shoemaker. You saved me from the dragon. I know my father has promised you my hand as the man who rescued me, and I shall abide by my father's wishes. But—"

The princess gasped as the shoemaker removed the cowl, revealing they were a woman. The shoemaker bowed to the princess and said, "But, Princess, I am no man, but a woman who has loved you from afar. When your father King Krak sent word that none of his knights had survived, I knew the time had come to take my chance. If you desire, I will take the gold offered and depart the kingdom, but if you so wish, I would be honored to wed you."

The crowd gasped. Sara blinked. Did the princess smile? Could the lips of a wooden puppet move that precisely? Was this a *sapphic* legend? In this small, religious town? Who was this puppeteer? The shoemaker and the princess kissing snapped Sara back to reality. The children and teens cheered, but the adults glared, looked away, and pulled their children from their seats.

Sara waited for the puppeteers to reveal themselves, and when the lone woman in a black dress and veil revealed herself, Sara applauded. The woman smiled from behind her veil as she bowed. Sara skipped toward her, pausing halfway, blushing, and shifting into a normal walk. The woman smelled faintly of roses but not normal roses. The rose scent had a dreamlike quality. Sara sneezed.

With a beaming smile on her face, she said, "Hi! I'm Sara, and I just caught the end of your show. You probably hear this all the time, but your puppets are so lifelike." She extended her hand, which startled Anya, who recoiled. Sara winced. "Not into touching, okay. Anyway, I loved your show."

Holding Iskra in her hands, Anya Skejik nodded. Her soft voice trembled in a tone just above a whisper. "Thank you. I am Anya. I have not seen you before."

Sara giggled and nodded. "I just moved into my great grandfather's house yesterday, Danforth Alexander the Fourth."

Anya nodded. "I think my father was his physician for a time."

"Oh, you're dad's a doctor? Mine makes bad business decisions. Anyway, are you hungry? There's some good food here, if you want to grab a bite."

Anya shook her head. "I have food at home, and they put meat in the food here."

Sara blinked. "You're a vegetarian too? I sort of noticed that, but the pantry was empty and the grocery store closed."

Iskra cleared her throat. "Aren't you forgetting something?"

"Sorry," Anya said. "This is Iskra. She's my first and favorite."

Iskra extended her hand. "It's a pleasure to meet you, Sara."

Sara smiled and shook the marionette's hand. "It's a pleasure to meet you too, Iskra. How long have you and Anya known each other?"

Anya blushed. She snapped the crossbar to silence the puppet, but Iskra said, "Since she was six-years-old."

The crowd moved to the square's edge as some of the men covered the cobblestones with large panels of varnished oak, connecting them with bolt latches. Musicians in traditional dress set up their performance area at the foot of the steps leading into the church. One had a single-stringed instrument with an almond-shaped body. Another had a fiddle. Others had pan pipes, a concertina, and assorted percussion.

"I heard there was a dance," Sara said. "I guess this is it."

Iskra nodded. She opened her wooden mouth to speak, but paused in shock as Anya said, "It's a traditional line-style dance from Europe, the Krest'yanskiy Tanets. All of us have learned it. It is time for us to pack the carriage and return home."

Sara nodded, paused, shook her head, and blinked. "You're not going to stay and dance?"

"I—no, I do not."

"What she's saying," Iskra interjected, "is that it's a partnered dance, and she—"

Before the marionette could finish the statement that caused Anya to blush, a middle-aged woman with brown hair and thick glasses wrapped her arms around Anya and Sara. Anya jumped. The woman said, "Well, looks like this will be a special Dożynki." She turned to the crowd and shouted, "Look, everyone! Dobrianya Skejik has a partner for the Krest'yanskiy Tanets!"

The crowd fell silent, and everyone turned in their direction. Anya lowered her head. She sucked in a breath and clenched her stomach muscles. Her foot tapped rapidly on the cobblestones. Sara looked at this woman and said, "But I don't know the dance."

The woman giggled. "Well, then Dobrianya here will have to lead." She turned to Anya and whispered through a smirk, "We'll let you get home by your bedtime." The woman laughed as she walked away.

"I won't force you to stay," Sara said.

"She's staying," Iskra said, leaning toward the dance floor. "Put me in the carriage where I can watch."

Anya nodded. She walked Iskra to the Skejik family carriage and placed her in the child's car seat, turning it so the marionette could observe the dance through the window. She returned to Sara and extended her hand, palm facing up. "If we are to do this, and only if you truly wish…"

Sara took the pause as an invitation and grabbed Anya's hand. A glottal gasp escaped Anya's mouth at the touch, and she released the breath she had held for the past few minutes. Sara's hand was soft. She wrapped her fingers around Anya's wrist and pulled her toward the other dancers, all of whom wore traditional attire. Observers whispered and mumbled, their eyes focused on Sara and Anya. Sara met every gaze with a broad smile, while Anya avoided them. When her eyes happened to meet Sara's, she jerked her gaze away.

The percussionist called the dance to order. Since she had to lead, Anya joined the line of men. The dance was lively and patterned. Its movements reminded Sara of the square dancing her middle school forced her to learn blended with the formal dances from Victorian and Edwardian period dramas. A few missteps happened as Anya adjusted to her role as lead, but after a dozen bars, the two danced in sync with each other and with the moves of the pairs around them.

The tempo plummeted on a downbeat. Anya closed the slender gap between them and encircled Sara's waist with her arm. Sara released a breath, and her shoulders relaxed the tension she didn't remember being present. In sweeping, waltz-like turns, they circled the dance floor. Sara's smile broadened and brightened with each revolution. And was that—yes—a tiny smile creeping onto Anya's face and shining through the veil.

The dance concluded and everyone clapped and cheered. Sara leaned close to Anya. "That was fun. Thank you."

Anya allowed her eyes to meet Sara's, her arm still wrapped around the blonde's waist. "It was pleasant. Yes."

Sara leaned closer. The lace veil wasn't opaque, but Anya's features were obscured enough it was hard to make them out. The world faded into a mist as the smell of roses rushed Sara's nostrils. No, it wasn't the smell of roses but of the memories of roses, like recalling how roses smelled in a dream, pleasant and familiar but terrifyingly unknown all at once.

Sara lifted a hand and touched Anya's cheek. The skin was smooth, slick, and warm. Strange. Anya stiffened and squeaked before sucking in a breath. She stepped back, her hands trembling, and darting her head between Sara and Iskra in the distance, she nodded. "I...I should head home before it gets late. Bye."

She disappeared into the crowd, and as the dreamy scent of roses faded from Sara's nostrils, the black carriage drove away to the north. Sara shrugged. "That was weird, still a good day."

4

Sara's Monday began with her usual run, but this time she woke an hour earlier to start her day. Why? The moving company was set to arrive this afternoon, and she wanted to make a grocery run before they arrived. She cursed herself for not even bringing oatmeal or Lucky Charms with her, so she had another breakfast of pierogies and coffee.

After her breakfast, she drove to Karelewski Grocers. The parking lot was smaller than she expected, but a handful of empty spaces remained. The store itself was small with two large single-pane windows flanking the wooden door. A green and white canvas awning provided shade. Through the windows, Sara saw the single cash register, staffed by an elderly woman with curly brown hair, and the first rows of shelves containing products as she approached the storefront. A bell jingled as she opened the door, and the cashier and Sara exchanged pleasant greetings.

Fifteen minutes of shopping later, Sara had filled her shopping cart with pantry staples, bread, homemade jams, as well as an assortment of apples, mushrooms, and vegetables, both fresh and frozen. As she perused the dairy cooler, the store owner, Harold Karelewski approached her. Tall and in possession of a dad bod, his salt and pepper hair had started to thin in the last few years, but his bushy beard and bright smile held people's attention. He wore his branded green and white grocer's apron over a brown work shirt and jeans.

"Finding everything you need?" His voice boomed without effort, filling the store.

Sara smiled. "Yes, sir. Just a few more things, and I'll be done. How are you today?"

"I'm well." His eyes surveyed her shopping cart. "We don't stock much meat, but if you head down the street to Barchek Butchers, they'll take good care of you."

"Thank you, but I'm a vegetarian." She grabbed milk, butter, and a block of smoked cheddar cheese. "But I'll keep that in mind for when I have company."

Harold nodded. "Or when a young suitor stays for supper, no?"

Sara snorted. "I doubt one of those will be around for a while."

"There are quite a few eligible bachelors here." The older man then leaned in close and whispered. "It might be better to keep away from Miss Skejik if you want to find an acceptable man."

Sara tilted her head. "She seemed like a nice person, maybe a bit of an introvert."

"You're new in town," he said. "She's a strange girl, keeps to herself and never talks to anyone, except through that puppet of hers. Acts like she's a real—er, like it's a real person."

"Oh? She spoke to me. Her voice was soft and gentle, but when the puppet spoke, she had a voice that sounded natural but way different. I don't know. What's...what's her story?"

Harold shrugged. "Don't really know. As young as she looks, I've always known her to live on her own. Parents killed themselves when she was a child, or so that's the story I always heard. She took over her grandfather's old toy store when she was sixteen. Can't say I have many memories of her, but she always smells like roses that are a little wrong." The smile returned to his face. "Well, I'll let you get back to your shopping. Just think about it, and welcome to Pazat."

"Thank you," Sara said, smiling.

She walked to the register and greeted the cashier. As the older woman started typing item SKUs into the register, Sara took several large canvas bags from her backpack and started bagging her own groceries. Taken aback, the cashier blinked. "That's a first," she said with a chuckle. "Most folks here just take the paper bags. The nice ones bring them back."

Sara shrugged. "When I moved out on my own, I got used to carrying groceries up two or three flights of stairs, so having good grocery bags became a necessity. Plus, it reduces waste."

The attendant looked up the SKU for the tomatoes. She nodded. "Can't say I blame you for that. How are you enjoying your new house? Is it as pretty on the inside as it is on the outside?"

Sara nodded and exhaled. "Oh, it's gorgeous. It's so much bigger than I expected."

"Oh, you did know Mister Alexander was rich, right?"

"Yes, ma'am. I did, but I never met him, honestly. Dad talked about him from time to time, but we never visited. Mom said he was a recluse."

The cashier's eyes shot wide. "A recluse? Danforth Alexander?" She burst into guffawing laughter. "Until he took ill a few years ago, that man was our mayor, always helping everyone in the fields, regularly hiking the mountains, and one of the best Krest'yanskiy Tanets dancers you'll ever find. After what you did yesterday, a proper teacher might make a dancer out of you too."

Sara blushed. "I had a lot of fun yesterday."

"Good," the cashier smiled. "Now, you just be careful. I don't know much about that Skejik girl, but she's a strange one."

"I've gotten the sense a lot of people think that, but she was friendly and nice to me. Mr. Karelewski said she lives by herself?"

The cashier's eyes darted from side to side. Seeing no one else was in this part of the grocery store, she leaned in close and whispered. "Well, along with that weird doll she talks through. Not her fault, poor girl. Her parents died when she was young—a car accident, mind you, or so I heard—but I also heard her father did things to her."

Sara's jaw fell, and her eyes widened. "No?"

"Oh, no, no, no." The cashier shook her hands. "I didn't mean like that. He collected old medical books from crackpot theorists and witches. Rumor is he experimented on her, and that's why she's a bit different. Their butler or grounds keeper, whatever he was, also died of like a serious bout of food poisoning or something. And she was close to him too. Poor thing. Well, your total is sixty-seven dollars and fifty-three cents. Will that be cash or check?"

"No card? I've got cash if not."

As Sara reached into her backpack and fished around for her wallet, the cashier said, "Until someone figures out why wireless and cellular services are so spotty, it's not reliable."

"Makes sense." Sara handed the woman the cash. "Here you go."

"Seventy dollars. Alright, that's two dollars and forty-seven cents in change. Here you go. You have a good day, and—oh!—get an electrician out there. Mister Alexander neglected some wiring issues when he took sick."

Sara nodded. "I will. Bye." She left the store and returned home.

After quick lunch of a grilled portabello mushroom burger, Sara confirmed the phone technician would arrive between two and six in the afternoon tomorrow to connect a wireless router. The lights flickered. It was an old house. The moving company was late, so she grabbed her copy of the *Caught in the Weaver's Dark Web* and sat on the brown leather sofa to read. The lights flickered and cracked. And then Sara's phone rang.

"Hey, Andrea," Sara said, laying the book face down on the sofa. "How's your semester starting?"

"There's a lot of static, Sara, but I think you asked about the semester? It's fine. One class period down, thirty-eight to go. How are you settling in?"

"I'm fine. The pace here is slow and relaxed. I'm glad they made me relinquish my assistantship. Apparently, Internet service here is spotty. I've got a tech coming tomorrow to set me up. But it's a cute town. I made it in time for their harvest festival!"

"Oh? What was that like?"

Sara tossed one leg over the sofa's arm and lay on her back. "It was fun. There was some procession of young girls in white nightgown-looking dresses going toward the church, and then there was food, a puppet show, some crafts for sale, and then a dance. I didn't know the steps, but it was fun to dance."

"Oh? Did some dashing young farmer's daughter ask you to dance?" Andrea laughed.

"No," Sara said. "She wasn't dashing. She seemed awkward and shy. And she wasn't a farmer's daughter. She's the town toymaker. She was tall and slender, and she smelled like roses from a dream."

"Roses from a dream?" Andrea's voice had a teasing quality to it, and she asked, "So what's this dream girl's name? Rosalind Ophelia Haversham?"

Sara blew Andrea a raspberry. "Her name is Anya. Anya Skejik, I think her last name is. She made the marionettes for the puppet show herself. I've never seen such realistic, intricate carvings and paintings on puppets. There was a dragon that breathed fire, and when it died, the puppet exploded into the audience. And in the end, the hero who saved the princess was a woman. I'll have to look up this folk tale, because it seemed to be a traditional story."

"You could always ask this Anya to tell you more about it when you invite her over for dinner."

Sara sputtered and coughed. She rose from the sofa and walked to the kitchen. "Why would I ask her out? We shared a few words and then danced. It wasn't like she asked me to dance. We were sort of teased into dancing together. It was clearly a festival thing."

"Of course, but hear me out. She told a folk tale that ended with two women living happily ever after *together*. Then when teased about a dance partner, she danced with you. It's all circumstantial, but I think you should talk to her."

Sara poured herself a glass of tap water. "I don't know. What would we talk about? What could I possibly have in common with this toymaker from a small town in the middle of the mountains that no one seems to know about? I mean, we like girls, and we're both vegetarians. That's about it."

"Oh, so you know she's a vegetarian. Not something I usually find out about random dance partners."

"I asked her if she was hungry, but she said she didn't eat meat. And then the dance started."

"So, you both seem interested in women being together, both are vegetarian, and both enjoy artistic endeavors. Yeah, nothing there to even have a conversation about over dinner."

Sara sipped the water. "Yeah, yeah, whatever. But you know I can't. She's got her own house and land apparently, and I have to stay in my great grandfather's—my—house for three years to give me time to figure out how to get out of that marriage clause. I can't fall in love. I can't chance it. She's too much of an introvert. So, there's that. Apparently, she doesn't talk to people without a going through a puppet. Not for me."

"And did you experience that?"

"Well," Sara paused and sighed. "She talked to me herself, and her voice was soft like her touch, gentle but sad. I wonder if she's lonely. The townsfolk say her parents died when she was like six or seven, I think, and she's been on her own since she was sixteen. But I've got my family to think about and my dissertation to figure out. Besides, you remember Donna, don't you?"

"You two made a cute couple until you broke up with her, that is."

Sara sighed. "Yeah, I really liked her, and she was cuddly and soft. We did have fun playing board games, and talking about books and movies."

"I remember," Andrea said. "Now why did you break up with her?"

Sara blushed sheepishly. "She didn't have a degree and had no desire to leave Nouvelle Arniers. I mean, it's a great city, but you know the academic life. We go where the jobs are. I would've had to break up with her eventually. This would end up the same. There's no point in trying." A moving truck pulled into the driveway. "The movers are here, Andrea. Let me let you go. I'll text you when I'm settled. Bye."

Skejik Toys was closed on Monday, not because Anya took the day to rest but because she spent the day in the back room preparing more toys. Tables, a workbench, and storage cabinets crowded the tiny room. Fabric scraps were draped over the Sears Commander sewing machine and over the back of the chair before it. Various doll parts in various stages of completion, littered the room. A dozen featureless porcelain heads sat around the edge of Anya's workbench, staring at her with their eyeless faces as she painted the button eyes on a plush rabbit.

Iskra watched from her seat beside Anya. Her lidless eyes observed the toymaker's work. "You think this one will sell? You spent a lot of money on that pink velveteen."

"I hope so," Anya said, holding up the completed stuffed animal. She smiled. "She's beautiful and so soft. I hope someone in need of comfort receives her."

The marionette nodded. "Masterful work, Anya. You've surpassed your mother and grandfather. Sure this one isn't for you?"

Anya held the rabbit close to her chest and then stroked the rabbit's cheek as she set it on the table beside her workbench. She grasped one of the doll heads and a paint brush. "Why do you ask that, Iskra?"

"You always keep the first toy you make after the Dożynki. That long hug you gave it before setting it on the table is telling. Plus, you've been lonely lately—lonelier than usual."

"I'm not lonely."

Iskra nodded once but remained silent. She watched as Anya colored the porcelain in a way that gave the face the appearance of being tanned. After an additional three coats, Anya was satisfied with the base skin tone. Anya used a silk cloth to dab more of the paint onto the skin, smoothing the complexion and adding nuance to the color, contouring the face to appear round with gently protruding cheekbones. Iskra nodded.

The marionette asked, "So, what was it you were doing this morning before breakfast?"

Anya paused, holding the brush vertically with pinkie extended. "I sat and observed the sunrise from the conservatory window. I've done that many mornings. Why?"

"You seemed more focused than usual. What caught your attention?"

"Something I haven't seen before, a person running without purpose through Pazat."

"Oh? And what about this running person drew your attention?"

Anya shook her head. "Nothing in particular. I've heard of people running for exercise but never seen it."

Iskra nodded. "Men do strange things. Surprised one of them drew your—"

"It was a woman." Anya's interruption was short and sharp. "It was the new woman in Pazat, Sara Alexander."

"Oh, it was. Wasn't it?"

Anya placed a dab of the glue into the empty left eye socket on the doll head. With a pair of silver tweezers, she took one green eye from a small jar and placed it over the dab of glue, sliding it until it was centered. She repeated the process with the other eye. Satisfied the eyes were even in both vertical and horizontal placement, Anya smiled.

She turned to Iskra and said, "Yes. Why do you bring it up?"

Iskra turned her gaze from Anya to the doll head in her hands. She shook her head and then looked up at Anya. "You've gazed out that window and watched the town below our home for years. People have walked and biked and driven through the streets, but you've never stared so intently that your porridge grew cold."

"I don't know what you're talking about." Anya shook her head. "It's not as if I was focusing on her, or the soft firmness of her hands."

"Never said it was, Anya."

Iskra focused her gaze on the toymaker's face as she glued a blonde wig on the doll head. With the hair in place, Anya screwed the head onto a metal stand. She turned to Iskra and said, "Good. Because I'm not thinking about her."

"Of course."

"And even if I were, nothing would come of it. Even I have heard the rumors surrounding her arrival. She has to remain in her great grandfather's home for three years and must marry an acceptable man, or she loses his fortune. I cannot be away from the grounds of our estate after midnight without risking death, and I am not a man."

"You don't know that you can't be away beyond midnight," Iskra said.

"But Papa said so. He said the medicine for my nervous condition tied me to the grounds of our estate, and if I strayed from our grounds beyond midnight, I would die. He called it an unfortunate side effect, but it's not so bad. Not that I want to be anywhere else."

Iskra raised her left hand. "She could move in with us, you know. Then, you wouldn't have to worry so much."

"As if she would do so, Iskra. She has a house almost as large as ours. And why would she want someone who can never leave? And if the stories from Mama's books are anything to go by, we have nothing in common. And again, I am not a man."

After giving the glue a few minutes to set, Anya took her grandfather's steel straight razor and began cutting and styling the hair. When she finished, the doll had an asymmetrical blonde bob. Anya smiled. She dabbed a few coats of sheer pink paint onto the lips. Once the paint had dried, she sprayed it with a paint setting spray, waited a few minutes, and then affixed it to the neck screw of one of her hand-carved wooden bodies with joints at the shoulders, elbows, wrists, hips, knees, and ankles.

"There," she said. "Now I just need to dress her. What do you think?"

Iskra appraised the masterfully crafted doll. "She's lovely, Anya. But, doesn't she remind you of anyone?"

Anya paused. Squinting, she turned a focused gaze to the doll. After a few minutes of examination, she shook her head. "No. I don't recognize anyone."

"Hm." Iskra nodded. "Maybe I'm seeing things then."

A week passed, and this week had been a series of struggles for Sara. The movers broke her full-length, free-standing mirror that was a present from her late grandmother. She was compensated the value of a similar item, but a new mirror could not replace the sentiment and memory. The phone company's technician spent five hours setting up high speed Internet access in the house, but the speed remained just above the fastest dial-up. At least the landline phone worked.

Now, on the afternoon of the first Monday in September, Sara plugged her cell phone into its charger and activated her personal hotspot. She powered on her laptop, which she connected to the Internet through her Ethernet cable. This was too important to leave to chance. The lights flickered.

"Fuck," she said. "Please don't die on me now, wiring."

The lights flickered once more, and that faint burning smell returned. Sara tensed. After a few moments of flickering, the lights calmed and functioned as normal. A relieved sigh escaped Sara's lips as she slid into the chair. She opened her Google calendar and clicked on the link connecting her to the scheduled Zoom meeting with Professor Hayes-Grey.

As the elder scholar's pixelated face focused on the screen, Sara smiled. The warning that her Internet connection was unstable flashed, but Sara ignored it and said, "Good afternoon, Professor. How are you doing?"

"As well as can be, Sara. I forgot to tell you I'm having surgery next week to remove an inguinal hernia, so I probably won't respond to emails for a month. But you keep working. How are you settling in at your new home?"

After a quick prayer to whichever deity controlled electrical wiring, Sara said, "Okay, I guess. It's a big change, and this town's really different from Nouvelle Arniers. But I'll make the best of..."

The now familiar thud of the circuit breaker tripping. All electricity in the house shut down. After a few seconds, the laptop detected the wireless hotspot and connected. Sara growled and shook her head.

"Sorry about that, Professor," she said. "The wiring is bad or something, and the circuit breaker keeps tripping. I've got an electrician coming out on Thursday to look at it. I forgot to unplug a few things to give me leeway."

Professor Hayes-Grey nodded. "Take care of that, Sara. You're a smart woman, but it's easy in grad school to forget life while working on your dissertation. And if the circuit breaker keeps tripping, that's a bad sign. Can I assume you haven't done any work on your dissertation?"

Sara shook her head. "Not as much as I wanted to. Once the electrician takes care of things, I'm going to head to New York for a few days to search the public and university libraries. I'm hoping that'll be next week. That way, when you're back from recovery, I'll have something big to show you!"

The elder scholar smiled. "Alright, Sara. That sounds good. Just be certain to have either evidence to support your claim or the outline and first chapter of your new direction. Okay?"

Sara nodded. "Yes, Professor. Hope your surgery goes well. Bye."

The Zoom meeting ended. Sara sank into the uncomfortable wooden chair. As her head fell over the chair's back, she sighed. *That went better than expected. Now, I just have to come up with something by next month.* Sara sighed. *Maybe I missed something in one of those articles.*

Sara perused the one hundred seventy-nine articles saved in her *Journal Articles* folder. Alphabetized by the last name of the lead author and further arranged by publication year, she mentally kicked herself for not subdividing them by whether or not the articles were cited in the current draft. She opened Alanzo Koetting's "Planting Doubts: Medical Ascendancy and the Demonization of Homeopathic Alchemy in Early Medical School Training". As she skimmed through the passages illuminated by her hightlighting and note taking, one brief passage between her annotations stood out.

When Samuel Hahnemann (1799) spoke of the <u>*Tincturam Magnae Animae*</u> *in Patacelsus'* <u>*De Mirabilibus,*</u> *he provided incorporated the scientific names of all ingredients in the Latin, with one exception. The Vysnívaná ruža, or the "Dream Rose," he presented in language of the Slovaks, as it was from an apothecary in Nitra who provided Paracelsus with his three seeds (Bentham 1829, pp. 17-21). In* <u>*De Mirabilibus,*</u> *Paracelsus (1529) described the Dream Rose as "possessing a subtle floral scent, akin to that of rose water, that lingers in the air and nose like an ancient dream one remembers dreaming but whose details one fails to recall" (p. 89). For the majority of those exposed to the scent or to tinctures including its essence, Paracelsus states that they exhibit a "brief but violent display of the conditions of their illness, followed by a peace wherein their affliction troubles them no longer" (pp. 91-92); however, there are extreme reactions in subsets of the population who experience vivid hallucinations that either lead to a worsening of their mental state or that border on spiritual ecstasy, which has led to their death at the hands of "lesser men with no understanding of the wonders this world produces when examined through the lens of True Scientific Inquiry" (p 92).*

"Some things haven't changed in five hundred years." Sara mused to herself as she stared at the words on her screen. Twenty minutes passed. An exasperated, whining growl whimpered through Sara's lips. She massaged her temples with the index finger and thumb of her right hand, sighed once more, and then slumped low into the chair. "I need to find a copy of *De Mirabilibus*. That's the only way my argument will work. Unless I shifted my focus to religious suppression of treatments for mental illness, but that still benefits from getting my hands on at least a facsimile of the Paracelsus text. Ugh. Why did I do this to myself?"

She wrinkled her nose and sniffed the air. "That damned burning smell is back. Let me go find as candle."

Sara went into the pantry where she stored her scented candles on a shelf built into the north wall. She selected a large candle in a textured blue glass jar, *Sea Salt and Ocean Spray*. She inhaled the candle's fresh scent and smiled. She set the candle on the coffee table in the sitting room, lit it, and sat on the sofa to finish *Caught in the Weaver's Dark Web* before heading upstairs for bed.

An unexpected burst of heat caused Sara to kick the duvet off of her in the early hours of Tuesday morning. She heard a thud, rolled over, and returned to sleep as the ceiling fan slowed to a stop. A few minutes passed, and the familiar burning smell paired with a fetid, sulfurous odor caused Sara's nose to twitch. She coughed but remained asleep. And then a repeated, screeching three-note siren blared through the night.

"The smoke alarm!" Sara's eyes shot open as she spoke. She bolted into a sitting position, and her eyes frantically scanned the room. No light meant no fire in her bedroom. The smell of burning filled the room, and the smell of smoke loomed in the distance. She threw on a tee shirt and a pair of pajama pants, grabbed her cell phone, and flipped the light switch. There was no electricity.

"Shit!"

Sara's hands trembled as she switched on her cell phone's flashlight. She raced into the hallway and saw smoke rising from under the door at the far end of the hall. Sara's eyes watered, and her heart quickened its pace. She sucked air into her lungs and held it as she raced down the stairs, grabbed her laptop and backpack, and exited the house.

Through quick, trembling breaths, Sara called emergency services. When the dispatcher answers, she said, "Hi. I'm Sara. My house is on fire. Help?"

"Oh, that's horrible. Now, first are you still in the house?"

Sara shook her head. "No. I ran outside."

"Good. I can't get a clear signal for your location. What's your address?"

Sara told the dispatcher her address and then added her phone number. She nodded as the dispatcher gave her information. The flames rose above her roof, sending light throughout the darkness. Tears choked Sara's voice as she said, "I just moved here. This was my great grandfather's house, and now..."

"Sara," the dispatcher said. "Sara, what matters is that you're safe. No one is in any immediate danger. A fire truck and an ambulance are en route. ETA is forty-three minutes. Local first responders are being alerted as well. Don't go back inside to get anything. Okay?"

"Yes. Okay. I'm not going anywhere."

"Good. Now, hold tight. I'm ending the call."

"Thank you."

The call ended, and Sara sank onto the dewy grass in her yard, watching as the flames spread through her house and thick clouds of black smoke rose into the lightening pre-dawn sky. As the roof crashed into the second story's floor, three pickup trucks sped into the parking lot. Men rushed from the trucks, grabbing pressure washers from the beds, and raced toward the house. Sara had spoken to some of these men throughout the last week, but her jaw still dropped as they soaked the exterior. One of the younger men ignored the others and opened the door, spraying the interior and moving slowly to stop the fire from spreading.

When the ambulance and fire truck arrived from Honesdale, the local citizens had the fire contained. The EMTs checked Sara's condition while the fire fighters quelled what remained of the fire. As dawn broke, several neighbors walked over to inspect the situation and check on Sara. Among them was Denis Novák.

He approached Sara with a sympathetic nod, looked to the remains of the house, and then said, "Electrical fire. You did call for an electrician as requested?"

Sara nodded. "Couldn't come until Wednesday. Guess there's no need for him to come now."

"You'll still need him," Denis said. "But there will be more services required. Funds will be drawn from the estate's finances, of course, should you choose to remain in the house, per the terms of the contract."

The Fire Marshal approached and said, "She can't stay in the house. Aside from the second floor having about twenty percent of the roof remaining, that entire floor is structurally unsound and the wires have been so chewed up with rats that she won't have electricity. The house has great bones, but it's a death trap right now."

"I understand," the attorney said. "However, there is the matter of her great grandfather's last will and testament. Should she not remain in the house for three years, the entire family will lose their inheritances. Should she leave, they might contest, and judges are fickle."

"If they contest, they stand to lose too, right?" The Fire Marshal pointed to the house. "If they're so keen on losing money, then let them fucking lose it. The young lady needs to live in a safe place."

Sara joined the conversation. "Isn't there a hotel or a bed and breakfast here I could stay in? Just until the house is repaired."

Denis Novák shook his head. "I'm afraid not. No one visits Pazat, so we've had no need." He paused and then sighed. "I suppose if you could find a place to live in Pazat, we could broadly interpret the terms of the will to allow for that, but I don't know where you'll stay."

The sound of hoof beats drew everyone's attention. They turned and saw the black Skejik family carriage pulled by the marionette horses. The carriage driver, another marionette, sat in silence atop the seat. Much of his carved face was hidden behind a wide-brimmed black hat and high-collared black coachman's coat. He extended his arm, holding an envelope sealed in wax to Sara.

With a shrug, Sara took and opened the envelope. The writing was in a stiff, unsteady hand.

Dear Miss Sara Alexander,

We sincerely hope this letter finds you alive and as well as can be during this period of transition and unexpected difficulty. From our window, we caught sight of the fire that attacked your home. While your situation is unique in its particulars, fires are neither uncommon nor unheard of in Pazat.

We have a proposition for you. The Skejik manor is large, and Dobrianya and I take up little space. As a result, we discussed the matter and wished to offer you the following: While your home is under repair and unlivable, we welcome you to join us during this time. The carriage will transport you and valued possessions.

Yours with sincerity,

Dobrianya Skejik and Iskra

"Well, that was weirdly worded," Sara said. "Looks like I've got a place to stay. Do you think I'll be able to grab a few clothes and things from the wreckage?"

The Fire Marshal sighed and shook his head. "Tell me specifics on where the items are, and I'll send my men in to retrieve them. They'll decide if it's safe to get them."

Sara nodded. Nearly an hour later, the firefighters brought one suitcase full of clothes, her doll and stuffed animal collection, the xBox, and Sara's collection of coffees and teas. They helped her load them into the carriage. The seating was covered in burgundy velvet with golden trim. Sara noticed a small box on the center of the floorboards with another note.

I've packed you a few snacks and some water. The trip isn't long, but you've been through a lot.

Anya

This note was in the same unsteady hand as the other note. Sara shrugged. The crusty bread slices, cheeses, and water were greatly appreciated. As the sun rose over Pazat, Sara peered outside the window as the carriage rolled through the town square. The fog, permeated by a faint smell of distant roses, picked up as the carriage passed Skejik Toys. Shadows formed in the fog. Sara blinked and rubbed her eyes. She shook her head.

I'm just tired and stressed from the fire. I swear I saw someone tall and thin with no face on his head. After I thank Anya for her generosity, I think I'll go to bed.

Once the carriage ascended the mountain, the smell of roses grew stronger but remained distant. Sara's jaw dropped as she saw the greenhouses that flanked the entrance to the Skejik manor. *I've had apartments smaller than those things.* The door to the carriage house opened, and the carriage entered. The door opened, and Anya, dressed in her standard black veil and dress, stood beside the door, Iskra in her hand. Sara smiled and moved to hug Anya, who tensed and stepped back.

"Sorry," Sara said. "I forgot you're not a hugger. Anyway, thank you so much for letting me stay here while my house gets fixed. I really appreciate it, and I won't be a bother. Honest."

Anya blinked. In her whispered voice, she started to speak, but Iskra interjected, "We thought it would be the least we could do, and Anya's getting tired of my company. Plus, you two seemed to hit it off at the dance."

Anya blushed. She turned her head to the side and regained her composure. "I'm not tired of your company, Iskra," she said. She bit her lower lip through the veil, released a breath, and then returned her veiled gaze to Sara. She smiled. "Sara, I am sorry about the fire, and you must be tired. Your possessions will be quite safe here, and the carriage house joins the manor, so you can retrieve them at your convenience. I will show you to your room, but then Iskra and I must head to the shop. We will return at six o'clock. Is this acceptable?"

Sara beamed. "I appreciate it, and yes, I could use a few more hours of sleep."

Anya nodded. "Follow me."

She led Sara into the house and up the stairs to a door. Anya turned to Sara and said, "If the furnishings are not to your liking, there are others in the linen closet. It has an adjoining bathroom. I will have a key made for you so you may come and go at your leisure. You are welcome to go throughout the house and the grounds, read the books in our library, and join us for meals, but that is not a requirement of you. I only ask that you do not go into my father's surgery room."

Sara nodded and yawned. "Thank you. I won't disturb the surgery. Don't think I would want to, so that's easy. And if there's anything you need me to do to help out around here, just ask. Thank you again."

Sara reached out and touched Anya's free hand. Anya gasped, and her cheeks flushed. She nodded. "Well, you rest, and we must tend to the shop."

With that, Anya bowed, and she and Iskra departed, leaving Sara alone in the Skejik family manor.

5

Sara woke from her sleep around noon. She yawned and rubbed her eyes. As her eyes focused, she bolted into a sitting position and gasped. This wasn't her bed, and this ruffled lavender bedding with yellow flowers around the edges wasn't hers. Her heart thundered in her chest. She looked around the room and saw shelves with books, toys, and dolls that she never owned. Why did the room smell like roses? No—not like roses but like someone had burnt a rose-scented candle in there a week ago but the scent lingered at the edge of perception. Her nose wrinkled, and her breathing quickened.

And then she saw the note from Anya. Or was it from Iskra? No, Iskra was a puppet, and so Anya used Iskra's voice for some reason. It was strange. After a long, slow exhale and another yawn, her muscles relaxed. A shiver ran up her spine. Even in September, the house felt cold.

Sara ran her fingers through her hair, wincing as she pulled on a knot. She yawned again. "I need coffee and a shower—in that order for my own safety."

Sara's jaw dropped as she walked to the kitchen. She hadn't seen one that spacious or that immaculate since she moved out of her parents' house at eighteen to start college. The vintage white appliances, the blue and white checkered paint on the cabinets that mirrored the marble tiles on the counter tops, and the subtle, soft glow from the yellow trim on the floorboards looked like something out of an antiques magazine. The searched the cupboards but found neither Keurig nor coffee pods. Sara frowned, and then she saw the French press sitting against the wall beside the stove. Oh well, morning coffee would take longer now.

Once the coffee had steeped long enough, Sara poured herself a cup and then added a splash of cream from the refrigerator. She made a mental note to make a pitcher of cold brew for tomorrow, but this would work for today. As she raised the warm cup to her lips, her cell phone rang. She narrowed her eyes when she saw her mother's name on the caller ID.

With a sigh, she answered. "Morning, Mom. What do you need?"

"Oh, so it's *What do you need* and not *How are you, Mom?* Well, I'm fine, Sara. Thank you for not asking. I get enough of that from your useless father. I don't need it from you too."

Sara sipped her coffee and then yawned into the phone. "Sorry, Mom."

"Yawning? At this hour of the day? What? It must be close to one in the afternoon. Have you been sleeping all day again?"

"No, Mom." Sara rolled her eyes. "I took a nap after getting to Anya's place, since my house in uninhabitable thanks to a fire."

"A fire? I told you not to burn so many candles. Now we're all going to be out of our inheritance, thanks to you."

"Jesus fucking Christ, Mom—"

"Don't you take the Lord's Son's holy name in vain, young lady! We raised you better than that. It's that liberal college brainwashing you."

Sara's gaze sank toward the table. "Sorry, Mom. I didn't do anything to destroy the house. It was an electrical fire that happened early this morning. And before you ask, an electrician was coming to look at the house tomorrow, but now most of the roof is gone. There's also serious electrical damage and damage to the second story floor and walls. And I can't live there, because the Fire Marshal came out and declared it unsafe until repaired. But I'm okay too."

"Yes. I'm glad you're fine, Sara. But what about our inheritance? You know the terms of your great grandfather's will, don't you?"

Sara sipped her coffee in silence. She sipped it again, and she sipped it a third time. She took a single, deep breath, and then she replied. "I am aware of them, Mom. And my attorney, who was both my great grandfather's attorney and the executor of his estate, has stated that he is confident that, given the circumstances, as long as I continue to reside in the town of Pazat, I am not violating the spirit of the directions. Thus, we are in good legal standing."

Sara then silently mouthed the words, *So there!* Her mother sighed. "I pray to God, Jesus, and all the angels in Heaven you're right. We need that money, since your stupid father took his month's money to the damned casino with those *investors* for his newest business idea. So, where are you staying again? At a hotel?"

"There are no hotels here, not even a bed and breakfast. But the town's toymaker, Anya—I think her last name's Skejik—a lot of Slavic names in this town. Anyway, she's letting me stay in her house with her while my place gets repaired. It's a bit drafty in here, but it's a nice house—*huge* house—for just her."

An exasperated sigh lurched through the speaker. "Sara Daphne Alexander, you know you have to look for a husband or we lose everything. I haven't spent years praying for you or sending you to that therapy camp that you ran away from to see you squander your chance to do something good for your family on some mountain town toy peddler."

"She's just a friend, Mom. I mean, I hope she considers me a friend. She's really nice and amazingly talented. She's just a little odd. It's not like I'm going to find anyone to date in this farming town."

Her mother's tone grew forceful and demanding. "You need to look for a husband, so put this toymaker out of your mind and focus on the task at hand."

"I've already told you there's nothing between us. Right now, I'm focused on fixing the house and finishing my dissertation. Speaking of, I need to call Mister Novák to see if there's a contractor he recommends."

"Fine, Sara. Just pray about what I said. You want to make us proud, don't you?"

"Sure thing, Mom. Bye."

Sara finished her coffee, washed and dried the French press and her cup, and went upstairs to take a shower. Sara chuckled, realizing she should have expected an elegant claw-foot bathtub instead of a shower. Sara knew she'd enjoy this tub more with a book and a bath bomb, but she had neither with her at present.

An hour later, Sara emerged from her bath, clad only in a lavender towel. Sitting on the bed, she surveyed the guest room. This was definitely a girl's room. It looked like it belonged to a more femme girl than Sara ever was. Everything was in lavender, yellow, pink, and white. A white lace tablecloth rested atop the small circular table beside the honey maple bookcase.

Sara walked over and examined the contents. The books looked old. Some had leather binding and some had textured cloth binding. Most appeared to be fairy tale compilations. Sara recognized the Grimms, Perrault, Afanasyev, and Anderson. A silver frame contained a photograph with two adults and a child. The child held a familiar doll. Sara smiled.

Must be Anya's family. Her mom was gorgeous. I wonder if she got her mother's eyes. It's hard to see through the veil. Look at little Anya in her lavender dress with the flower crown in her hair and that huge smile on her face. Sara sighed. *She seems so sad now, but I guess losing your parents will do that to you.*

As she returned the photograph to its place on the shelf, she noticed a worn leather book hidden behind it. Thinking it to be a well-loved classic, Sara grabbed the tome as she set the photograph in its original place. Sara flipped through the pages, filled with a neat, flowing script as well as pen sketches of flowers, people, and animals. This had to be a diary. Could it be Anya's? Who else's could it be? Sara paused, but after a minute, curiosity won. The pen sketch of the town's school house suggested this was from sometime during the school year.

August 25

Dear Diary,

Tomorrow, I start school and get to meet other children. Well, I've met a few of them when they came into Dziadzio's shop. But most didn't talk to me, and I heard them tell their mommies I was stinky. I don't know why they said that, because I bathe twice each day, wear perfume, and use the deodorant stick Mama buys from

Karelewski's store. Papa says they're reacting to the medicine he gives me to keep me well. He says some people smell the medicine in people's skin, and they find the smell unpleasant. Mama says people are the same way with different perfumes.

I hope I make some friends. Papa works a lot keeping people well, but he's always in his lab making medicines for me and other people. I don't get to see him except after supper, when he reads fairy tales to me and helps me with my writing and arithmetic. Mama is helping Dziadzio at the toy shop, and she lets me go with her some days. But most days, I play with Mikhail, and he's older than Papa.

Well, Diary, Mama will be here soon to tuck me in and kiss my forehead. I'll tell you all about my first day of school tomorrow. Night night.

Sara turned the page to the next entry and paused. *No, I promised only one entry. I shouldn't keep reading. Anya would tell me if she wanted me to know.* Sara returned the diary to the shelf, carefully placing it behind the family photograph. She then dressed and searched for the library.

While Sara spoke with her mother, Anya placed the *Closed for Lunch* sign in the window of Skejik Toys. She returned to her workroom, where she had completed three dolls and had begun painting the pieces of a puzzle. "Well, let's go home for lunch, Iskra."

The marionette lifted her chin to meet Anya's gaze. "It's already half past twelve. If we go home, we won't get back to the shop until three. Why don't you just head to Karrolton's Café? I'll stay here."

Panic livened Anya's face. She shook her head in short, rapid bursts. "No. No. I can't be without you. How will I talk to these people?"

Iskra tilted her head to the left and then to the right. She raised her hands. "You manage to talk to Sara without my help."

Anya turned her gaze to look away from the marionette. "I don't know what you mean. You're the one who wrote the note and sent the carriage to her home. I was unaware of you doing that, by the way."

"Did you forget what happened after you listened to me and made that one change to the legend of the Wawel dragon? You two talked for five minutes before you signaled me to take over for you."

Anya shook her head. "She caught me off guard. That is all, Iskra." She picked up the marionette and walked toward the rear door. "Come on. Let's go."

The shining sun warmed the air. Pazat's normal fog had thinned almost to the point of disappearing. A handful of adults milled about the town square. They greeted Anya but kept a noticeable distance. She either nodded in response or directed Iskra to respond.

"Oh, look," Iskra said. "A week ago you danced and talked with a stranger, interacting with another adult without me in your arms."

A flash of heat reddened Anya's cheeks. She swallowed hard and then shrugged. "Sara is new to Pazat. I was being a good neighbor."

Iskra rolled her eyes. "And that's why you spent the last week crafting a porcelain doll in her likeness, right?"

Anya paused. She lifted her gaze and pressed her tongue against the inside of her cheek. After a moment, she tilted her head and then shook it in dissent. "I don't see the resemblance."

Karrolton's Café was the only restaurant in Pazat. Although its name suggested dainty and elegant fare, both the interior and the menu had more in common with a classic, American diner. Green and white tiles covered the floor, and a dozen booths with green leather upholstery lined the walls of the small restaurant. Sara wrinkled her nose at the smells of sausage, onion, pepper, and beef that filled the air. The grill sizzled, and the coffee percolators rumbled as they brewed fresh coffee.

A handful of patrons turned as Anya entered. Their gazes followed her as she walked to the end of the bar and sat on the first stool. The nearest patron, who sat three stools over, wrinkled his nose and then slid two more stools away from her. One of the servers, a young brunette, refilled the coffee cup for an old man who sat in the booth against the wall, sipping his coffee and reading a newspaper, approached her with a nervous smile.

"Good afternoon, Miss Skejik," the young woman said. Her nose wrinkled. She sneezed. "Excuse me. Will you be dining in this time?"

Anya shook her head. Iskra turned her face toward Anya and nudged her. Anya nudged the marionette to speak, but she remained silent. Anya narrowed her eyes and sighed. She shook her head again.

The young woman rolled her eyes and nodded. "Ah, I see. Will you have your usual? Oh! We also have some nice potato, onion, and bell pepper stuffed cabbage rolls. I think you'd really like them."

Anya flicked her wrist, but Iskra remained silent. Anya flicked her wrist again. The doll refused to speak. Anya grumbled as she flicked her wrist a third time. The doll remained steadfast in her silence. The server looked away and flicked her tongue against her teeth. Anya sighed. In a voice that was a hush above a whisper, she said, "The cabbage rolls."

The server blinked. She looked around, an inquisitive look on her face, but no patron made eye contact. She gasped and returned her attention to Anya. "Sorry about that, but did you say the cabbage rolls?"

Anya nodded. She opened her mouth to speak, but Iskra chimed in, saying, "Yes, she did. She's changing things up today."

The server blinked three times. She nodded. "Yes, of course. Yes, ma'am. I'll have those right up. It'll just be a few minutes. Okay?"

Anya nodded. The server filled out the paper ticket, placed it on the pass, and rang the bell. "Order!"

While Anya waited in silence, a middle-aged brunette with thick glasses framing her hazel eyes entered the restaurant. A sly smile slid over her round face as she slipped onto the stool beside Anya. Looking toward the toymaker, her voice sounded like a conspiratorial stage whisper when she said, "Hello, Anya Skejik. I see you've moved fast. That new girl in town is already living with you. Or maybe she made the first move. Huh?"

Anya fixed her gaze upon the slice of the kitchen visible through the pass. After a pleading wrist flick, Iskra said, "Well, Nancy, we saw her house catch on fire from our window, and we thought instead of introducing ourselves when she moved in and then let her suffer, we decided to show honor and hospitality. Why do you insinuate something more?"

Anya released a held breath and relaxed the tension in her shoulders she didn't realize she carried. Nancy flattened her smile into pursed lips. She offered a single, slow nod. "I see." She paused for a moment before saying, "Well, you've always been a strange little thing with peculiar interests. My Carolyn noticed it when you were a child along with that *odor* that always follows you."

"I guess you've never had anyone give you a rose then," Iskra said. "You were probably called one because of your thorny personality."

Nancy hissed as she spat her next words. "At least my Carolyn and I can speak to adults without hiding behind a toy."

At that moment, the server walked up with a brown paper bag. She smiled at Nancy and then said, "Oh, hi, Miss Sullivan. I'll be with you in a second." She turned to Anya. "Here you go, Miss Skejik. That'll be nine dollars and seventy-two cents."

Anya handed her a ten-dollar bill and then said, "Keep the change. Thank you."

With her eyes closed, Anya rose from her stool, grabbed the bag with her empty hand, and then left the restaurant.

Exhausted from the stress of the fire and her conversation with her mother, Sara excused herself after supper. She returned to her room and locked the door behind her. Her eyes darted from side to side and from the floor to the ceiling. The room had no HVAC vents, using a radiator to heat the room as needed. She removed her clothing, tossing it onto the chair by the bookcase. Confident in her security, she slipped Anya's diary from its hiding place, walked into the adjoining bathroom, and drew herself a bath.

As the steam rose from the tub and filled the bathroom, Sara stared at the diary. "Why are you doing this, Sara Daphne? Remember how you hurled books at Dave when he read yours to all his friends while they played video games at a sleepover?" Sara sighed as she fixed her hair in a bun to keep most of it out of the water. "I just need to know more about her for some reason. And she's a private person, so I can't just ask her. Not like she would volunteer any information either. So, the diary it is."

A series of thumps sounding on the floor from the bedroom. Sara's head jerked. She placed the diary on the toilet bowl lid and peeked through the door. Nothing. Sara shook her head. This was an old house, so it was probably the floorboards settling. Sara sighed and shook her head before closing the door and slipping into the hot bath. She opened Anya's diary to two entries after the one she read earlier and read.

August 27

Dear Diary,

I made two friends today! Carolyn Sullivan demanded Damian Rabinowicz switch seats with her so she could sit next to me. Her family moved into Pazat ten years ago. She has blonde hair and blue eyes, and she wore a red dress with a black belt.

Remember how everyone moved away from me yesterday and said I smelled funny? Carolyn doesn't seem to have the bad feelings about the smell from the medicine Papa gives me . She said I smelled like the tulips her Baba plants in her garden back in Philadelphia. That's weird, since Papa uses his special roses in the medicine.

At lunch, she introduced me to a friend of hers, Lida Petska. Lida talked less than I did, and she always agreed with whatever Carolyn wanted. But I have friends now! Mama said she and Dziadzio will make special toys for their birthdays.

I'm about to go take a bath, and then Mama will read me a bedtime story. I can read now, but I like it when she reads to me. I hope she'll always be around to read to me.

The thuds returned, and this time, they sounded patterned. Sara closed the diary and fixed her gaze on the bathroom door. "Hello? Anya? Is that you?"

The sounds stopped. No one answered. Sara shrugged. "Well, I don't want to read everything, so let's skip a few entries." She thumbed through the pages until the first line of an entry caused her eyebrow to raise. "This should be interesting."

September 17th

Dear Diary,

I take back everything I've said about Carolyn! I was supposed to go spend the night at her house, but after what she did at school today, I'm not going. Jessica and Candace Hoff chased me into the bathroom, calling me Stinky Skejic, while everyone laughed and cheered. I ran into a stall and hid, sitting on one of the toilets and keeping my feet out of sight.

While Jessica and Candace banged on the door and chanted, I cried and begged them to stop. Suddenly, Carolyn poked her head under the stall. She asked if I wanted help, and I told her I did. She nodded and smiled.

A few seconds later, I felt water on my head. I looked up and saw a bucket tilting over the edge of the stall. My nose wrinkled as its stinky liquid soaked me. And then I felt a soft, moist poop log slapped me in the face. I felt sick, and then I saw Carolyn's face looking down on me and laughing. She said now I smelled better than ever. Everyone laughed. I thought she was my friend.

Crying, I ran to Mama and Dziadzio's shop. Mama hugged me, even though I stank and was covered in poop and dirty water. She took me home and helped me clean up. I don't want to go back to school again, but I know I have to.

The entry continued, but Sara stopped reading. With her eyes wide, she pushed a long, slow breath from her lips. Sara closed her eyes and sighed. Closing the diary, she set the book on the toilet. She sank into the tub. The room temperature water chilled her skin. Sara stretched her leg and flicked the faucet knob, adding more hot water to the tub.

After a moment of silence, Sara ran her fingers along the tub's smooth edge. She nodded three times. *Damn*, she mused silently. *From what I've heard about Anya's parents, this must've been in either kindergarten or first grade. What a way to start a school year. I just want to hug her after this, but I know she doesn't like physical touch. She's not weird. She's...lonely.*

"She's lonely." The refrain escaped Sara's lips in whisper.

The lights flickered. Sara jerked upright into a sitting position. Her chest rose and fell with quick breaths. A heavy thunk pounded the floor in the bedroom. Sara's head turned toward the door, her right eyebrow lifted inquisitively. After a minute, a quick series of lighter thumps pattered across the floor. Someone was in Sara's room.

Sara rose from the tub, grabbed the towel, and wrapped it around her body. Water dripped from her body as she crept forward, and wet footprints marked her path. A door opened and then closed. She opened the bathroom door and poked her head into the bedroom.

No one was in the room. Sara's eyes darted from left to right as her head scanned the room. Her heartbeat echoed in her ears. She swallowed hard, took a deep breath, and then stepped furtively into the bedroom. Looking around, her backpack was on the floor, and her wallet had fallen out. Sara shrugged. She thought she zipped it up, but maybe she didn't.

As Sara returned to the bathroom to prepare for bed, Iskra moved through the hallway away from Sara's bedroom. The strings controlling the puppet dragged behind her on the floorboards as she walked toward the library. Reading a book she selected from the thousands filling the floor-to-ceiling cases, Anya sat curled up in one of the oversize brown leather chairs, a cup of tea beside her on an octagonal mahogany table. "I'm back," the marionette said, her voice taking on a melodic tone.

Anya lifted her gaze from her book. "Back? Where did you go?"

"Oh, just gathering a little information, since you're not in a chatty mood."

Anya turned the page in her book and then sipped her tea. "So what did you learn?"

Iskra raised her hands and shrugged. "Not much. Her computer was too heavy to lift, but her birthday is in eight days."

"Are you suggesting we throw her a party?" Anya tensed her shoulders and drew her arms and legs into her body as she asked the question, her eyes never leaving the page of the book she was reading.

Iskra's eyes rolled. "If you're up for a gossip-worthy social event, sure, but that might mean inviting people to the house. Oh, don't cringe so hard. You have to learn to talk to people eventually. You could, however, surprise her with a thoughtful gift. Seems she has a pretty extensive doll and stuffed animal collection, and you happen to be a talented toymaker who…"

"Could craft the perfect doll to fit the aesthetic of her collection."

Iskra stared at Anya for a moment, and then the doll's eyes blinked once. "Sure. Or you could give her that doll you made that looks remarkably like her."

"The blonde one I made earlier? You still believe it resembles Sara? I don't see it, but if you think she would enjoy that one, Iskra, I trust your judgment. I suppose we should bake her a cake as well."

"Now you're thinking. But it's getting late. Set your book down, and let's go to bed."

Anya nodded and smiled. "Yes. Thank you, Iskra. You've always been so good to me. Mama poured enough of her spirit into you when she made you that it almost feels like she is with me still."

Anya closed her book, L. E. Stapleton's *By Blood and Vine*, on the side table. Taking the tea cup and saucer in one hand and cradling Iskra with her other arm, Anya left the library, returned the cup and saucer to the kitchen for morning washing, and began her bedtime routine.

6

Sara spent the next four days working with contractors, subcontractors, and the electrician she had hired to repair the house. None of them felt the work would be difficult, but the electrical work would be extensive, given both the fire damage and the number of wires needing to be replaced as rats had chewed through them. Including her requested updates to the HVAC and electrical systems, the contractor estimated the repairs should require between six and eight weeks, weather permitting.

After meeting with her attorney on Friday afternoon, Sara decided to make her first visit to Skejik Toys. As she walked through the town square, a young brunette waved as she approached. Sara smiled and waved. "Hi, Melana. Off to work?"

The young woman nodded. "Yes, ma'am, Miss Alexander—er, *Sara*. You coming by for a snack while you wait for Miss Skejik to finish working?"

"Oh? It's a cool shop, if the smell doesn't overwhelm you."

"Smell?" Sara tilted her head to the side as she spoke and then scratched her scalp.

"Yeah, that weird rose smell, like roses in another room. Some people like it, but others really hate it. It gives me a headache if I'm in there too long, kind of like when someone smokes marijuana or burns sage. But what she can do is amazing. I mean, you've seen the mechanical horses that pull the carriage. That's all her work."

Sara nodded quickly. "I almost thought the carriage driver was a real person when I first interacted with it, but that was at four in the morning after my house caught on fire. But she insists I take the carriage into town, even though it means she walks to work."

Melana shook her head. "She always walks. Okay, I've seen the carriage in town if it's raining or if she needs to get groceries. She just likes to walk. Must be good exercise." The younger woman looked around and then leaned in close. She whispered, "This may seem rude, but have you ever seen her face? Without the veil, I mean."

Sara shook her head. "She gets up before I do, and when I get up, she has it on. She eats with it on. It's not opaque, so I've seen the outline. At the harvest festival, I slipped my hand under her veil and felt her face. It was smoother and warmer than I expected. Why?"

Melana shrugged. "Curiosity. I mean, you've heard about the burns, right?"

Sara blinked. "No. She was burned?"

"That's the story. Something happened when she was a kid and half her face was burned. I don't think I'm more than ten years younger than she is, but everyone—even my grandpa—tells stories about it like it happened ages ago. Anyway, I've got to get to work. If you get hungry, you know where we are!"

Sara chuckled. "I will, Melana. Thank you. Have a good shift."

When Sara opened the door to Skejik Toys, the doorbell rang. The pleasant scent of distant, hazy roses filled the air. Iskra's voice called out from her perch beside the register. "Welcome to Skejik Toys! Dobrianya Skejik will be with you in a—oh, hi, Sara!"

"Hey, Iskra. It's just me. Tell Anya not to stop whatever she's working on."

"Just you? *Just* you? You're the first guest we've had at the Skejik manor in decades."

Sara blushed. The marionette's voice sounded closer than expected. Sara blinked. Iskra had moved to the table just in front of her. But that was impossible with Anya in the back workroom. Wasn't it? Sara must've assumed Iskra was by the register, and the store must have a PA system with individualized speakers.

Anya emerged from her workroom. "Hi, Sara. How was your meeting?"

Sara sucked a quick breath into her lungs. *She asked about my day! She always does, but she usually waits until I mention it.* After biting her lower lip, Sara beamed and said, "It was what I expected. Money's still coming in like it should, which makes my family happy, and he's found precedent to quell any will contestations should they happen while I'm staying with you. Also, the repairs are progressing as expected, so that's good. Again, thank you so much for letting me stay with you. I don't know what I would've done otherwise."

Iskra raised her hand and started to speak, only to have Anya interrupt her first syllable. "I have found it pleasant to have you in my be—in my home."

Sara bounced on her heels and beamed. "I know you're a private person, so I really appreciate it. And I'm glad I'm not a burden. I know you're not finished working, but I wanted to come and see the shop at least."

Anya nodded. "Feel free to look around. It's a small shop, but it's mine. I have a piece to finish, but you can watch if it won't bore you."

Iskra's gaze shifted from Anya to Sara and back to Anya while the toymaker spoke. The marionette shrugged, confused as to what had just happened.

"I don't want to disturb you," Sara said, a wide smile illuminating her face. "I'll be super quiet if I join you. Want me to bring Iskra in the back when or if I join you?"

Iskra nodded. "Yeah, I'm tired. I don't feel like walking any more."

The marionette yawned and stretched her limbs. Sara giggled. "Okay then. I'll have a look around and then head back."

Anya nodded and returned to her work in the back room. Sara paused. Her head tilted to the right, and her gaze shifted toward the ceiling. *What did I just ask? Puppets don't move on their own. But I swear it was by the register when I entered. But it's cute.*

Sara walked around the store's showroom. Her eyes sparkled joyfully as she looked at the dolls, stuffed animals, and carved wooden toys. She picked up two of the tin soldiers, whistled, and ran her index finger along every groove and indentation.

Does she make everything? She mused, observing the faces of three different soldiers. *It's all so detailed. And these soldiers all have individual faces, unique expressions, hairstyles, eye colors. That can't be from a mold, can it?"*

"Do you sculpt the tin soldiers," Sara asked, raising her voice just enough to reach the back room.

"Nope," Iskra responded as if she were behind Sara.

Sara turned toward the sound and saw the marionette sitting on the shelf attached to the wall. Sara jumped and yelped. She blinked, and Iskra had disappeared. Her heart and breathing quickening, Sara looked about the showroom. There Iskra sat in her perch beside the register. Sara shook her head. What was happening?

"Dziadio made the molds," Anya said from the workroom. "I believe the English word is *granddad*, if that helps. I use his molds, but the painting is mine."

Sara nodded. After a few more minutes wandering around the store, she made her way to the workroom. Anya sat at the large table with a yardstick built into one edge. The naked wooden body of a porcelain doll she had recently carved sat in front of her as she embroidered a floral pattern around the collar and hem of a vest. The doll's face was meticulously carved, but the slight imperfections of one eye being just a hair's width higher than the other, a crooked smile, and a slight double chin resembling baby fat gave the face a realistic appearance. When the brown eyes caught the light at the right angle, the gold and scarlet inflections gave these plastic—or maybe glass—eyes a realistic appearance.

Anya's focused gaze peeked through the side of her veil. She sucked her cheeks in and pursed her lips, revealing the gentle curve of bone structure. The high collar of her black dress hid her neck, but the precision of its fit displayed the elegant curve of her shoulders. Sara smiled.

A few minutes of silence passed before Anya paused. She turned to the side, and her eyes met Sara's. "Is something wrong," Anya asked.

"No, why?"

"You have this smile on your face. You smile often, but this one is different."

Sara blushed. She shook her head rapidly. "Just my normal smile. Yes, my normal smile when watching someone do amazing work."

Anya smiled. "Thank you then. I should finish soon, and we can return home."

Sara watched in rapt attention as Anya finished the vest and then dressed the doll in the vest, blouse, skirt, and shoes. She set the doll on a dolly loaded with other dolls and stuffed animals. As Anya tidied her work area, Sara asked, "Are these dolls going to the showroom? I can wheel the dolly out there for you when I go pick up Iskra."

"These have already been sold. A distributor named Franz Schwartz has purchased our dolls and stuffies since my mother was a child. He places one order each quarter for two dozen pieces to sell through his own store and his catalog."

"F. Schwartz and Sons," Sara said. "My parents have bought me several toys and dolls from their catalog. Heck, I've bought stuff from them in the past few years. They're not inexpensive. How do people here afford your work?"

Anya wiped down the table. "They are charged less here. Mister Schwartz adds his own markup to turn a profit. I price things at a reasonable rate here. We do well enough on our own, but the Schwartz sale is valuable."

"I bet," Sara said. "Well, let me go grab Isk—Ah! When did you—*how* did you—get here?"

Sitting on the edge of the table, Iskra said, "I'm silent like a ghost in the night."

"She is," Anya said. "I forgot to tell you, forgive me. I've grown accustomed to it."

Sara paused for a moment. That was a strange thing to say. She shrugged. "And your mother made her for you, you said?"

Anya nodded. "When they pulled me from the school and taught me at home. Well, it's time to close shop and return home. Will you join me in the garden to select vegetables for tonight's meal?"

Sara smiled. "I'd love to."

Once they returned to the Skejik Manor, Sara and Anya dropped Iskra off in the den. At the puppet's request, Anya switched on the television, allowing Iskra to watch *Jeopardy*. As Ken Jennings introduced the first round of categories, the two young women left the manor and walked to the greenhouse used to provide vegetables and herbs for the family's meals.

Sara expelled a long, slow breath that sounded like the word wow as she surveyed the dozen meticulously even rows of vegetables and herbs, each labeled with the English name, the biological name, and a photograph. Basil, sage, oregano, and rosemary perfumed the sweltering air.

As she inhaled the rosemary's woodsy aroma, Sara smiled and said, "I grew up privileged, but I've had apartments smaller than this greenhouse. And you've got two of them."

"The other contains flowers and other plants Papa used in making medicines," Anya said, grabbing one of the wooden baskets. She pulled two garlic plants from the soil and placing them in the basket.

"He was a doctor, right? Or was he some kind of herbalist?" Sara grabbed a plump tomato from the vine. "These tomatoes look great. We could make a sauce for some pasta."

"Pick a dozen, please," Anya said, nodding. "And yes, he was a physician, but he also employed herbal and homeopathic cures. Some patients preferred them. Others could not afford the medicines otherwise. And sometimes the shipments from the pharmacies did not arrive in a timely manner. Did we hear the gossip correctly? Are you studying to become a doctor?"

Sara's face scrunched. She shook her head but then nodded. "No but yes. I'm going be a doctor, but a doctor of philosophy, not a physician. But I'm studying the history of medicine. My argument is that Samuel Hahnemann's homeopathic thesis would have been applicable to mental illness, as he proposed in his diary, but he references a text by Paracelsus that appears to have been lost. I've read a handful of scholars who've cited the text, mostly by secondary citations, but no one seems to have a copy of the text. And without it, I'm screwed."

"I'm sorry." Anya placed three white onions, a handful of carrots, and a dozen mushrooms of various types into the basket. "What text is it? And if people know of it, why can't anyone find it?"

"*De Mirabilibus Occultis Naturae*. I mean, it happens with these manuscripts that are like a few centuries old. They burn in fires, get stolen, damaged, lost during renovations. Stuff happens, and since there probably weren't that many copies to begin with, the loss of one always has the potential to mean no more copies exist. It's a tragedy how easy it can be to lose art, knowledge, and...." Sara paused before gasping and then adding, "...history."

Sara glanced down. Anya had placed her soft hand atop Sara's. Sara blushed and bit her lip. Her heart quivered. Anya said, "Don't lose hope. Answers come when needed most. When I needed a friend, Mama introduced me to Iskra, and she's been a friend, confidant, and guide throughout my life. I can feel Mama's love when I hold her. Maybe something good will come to you soon."

She touched me. Sara swallowed hard and then released a breath she didn't know she was holding. She nodded and then smiled. "Maybe. I hope so."

Anya nodded. "Well, let's pick some herbs and then start supper. We'll have to make the pasta from scratch."

Sara beamed. "I can do that while you prep the sauce."

Anya smiled, and they left the greenhouse and returned to the manor.

Dense, soupy fog blanketed Pazat on Tuesday, muting the dawn song of the local birds. Dark clouds filled the sky. Anya had already left for work when Sara awoke, yawning and groaning. She looked out the window, groaned, and rolled over. Her alarm sounded, and she slapped the phone into silence. Her snores drowned out the text message vibrations that pinged repeatedly over the next seven minutes.

A series of six thumps knocked on the bedroom door. Sara mumbled a barely audible, "Go away. It's too foggy."

Three more knocks sounded. Sara ignored them as she slept. Her cell phone vibrated from another text message. There was another knock on the door. The snooze alarm sounded. The phone flipped onto its screen and leaped off the nightstand, slamming into the wall. Sara gasped and sat up in bed. She yawned, blinked, and rubbed her eyes.

Looking around the room, Sara saw her phone on the floor by the wall. She shook her head and shrugged. "Don't remember hitting it that hard."

Sara moaned as she arched her back. After getting out of bed, she looked around for the tank top and pajama pants she wore when lounging. A few minutes passed before she realized she had slept in them. Sleeping nude was her preference, but when she was a guest in someone's home, she always wore clothes to bed.

Shaking her head, Sara picked up her cell phone and scanned the missed calls and texts as she walked toward the bathroom. "Mom, Mom again, oh and Mom a third time. Well, she can wait until after my shower." Sara tossed her phone on the bed and walked into the bathroom.

After showering, Sara sat on the bed and called her mom. "Hi, Mom. Sorry I slept through your call. I've been sleepier than usual this past week."

"Are you alone?" Her mother's tone was sharp and harsh.

"I think so." Sara scratched the back of her neck. "Anya's usually at her shop at this time, and there's no one else here. Why?"

"Because you're packing your things and going somewhere else. You are not staying with that freak."

Sara's face contorted in confusion. "Huh?"

"Pack your things. Don't give me that look I know you have on your face, Sara Daphne. I've done some digging on this person you're staying with. Did you know she doesn't even go to church?"

Sara rolled her eyes and then feigned shock with a gasp. "No? Really? That's so unlike me who...also doesn't attend church. Where would I go?"

"Don't you mock me. I hoped moving away from that sinful city and its liberal university would help you move out of that phase you've been in—"

"Not a phase, Mom."

"Anyway, I had her investigated, and she doesn't go anywhere. She doesn't talk to people. Apparently, she only talks to this doll. That's serial killer behavior, and we don't need you getting killed until you find yourself a husband."

Sara sighed. She pursed her lips. "Anya is not a serial killer. And there's not really anything to do in this town, so why would she go anywhere? She's quirky, sure, but she's an amazing artist. Did you know she sells the dolls and plushies she makes to F. Schwartz and Sons? According to their online catalog, Blinsky & Skejik dolls sell for three hundred a piece! I'm surprised I don't have one of her dolls, as many as I've bought over the years. And she talks to me. Her voice is—was—sad, but it seems lighter now."

Sara smiled. Her feet trembled in excitement. Her mother cleared her throat. "This is not how we raised you, Sara. As if being a backsliding lesbian wasn't enough, you fall in love with a serial killer."

"She's not a serial killer, Mom. And I haven't fallen in love with her, not that it's a bad thing if I did. She's kind. She's sweet. She has her own garden so she can eat vegetarian food all year long. She has her own house, and she built the mechanism that moves her carriage. She's amazing. But we're just friends. I think we're friends. I hope she sees me as a friend."

As Sara opened her mouth to start her next sentence, her mother said, "Well, you better keep it that way. Don't you ruin this for your family, Sara. Now, I've got to get to my cardiologist. Love you."

"Love you too, Mom. Bye." The call ended.

Sara passed the day reading and rereading journal articles she downloaded, breaking only for lunch, until Anya returned home and prepared supper. After that, she joined Anya in the library while Iskra remained in the sitting room to watch *Jeopardy*. As Sara settled into one of the two massive armchairs, Anya opened the wooden globe beside the leather sofa, revealing a crystal decanter and three sets of four crystal glasses, one set for red wine, one set for white wine, and one set of rocks glasses.

"Would you like a glass of wine," Anya asked. "It's a Pinot Noir. I opened it yesterday evening, and it's rather nice."

"I didn't know you drank," Sara said. "Sure."

Anya poured two glasses and then handed Sara one. "I rarely indulge, but as you joined me tonight, I thought it reason to cele—uh, I thought I would offer."

Her face reddened behind the veil. Sara sipped the wine, tasting the cherry, vanilla, and warm baking spice notes. "This is nice. And I wanted to, but you came across as a super private person. I didn't want to impose."

Sara caught the faintest glimpse of Anya's smile as her veil swayed when she sat in the other armchair. "You are not incorrect. However, it has been pleasant having you stay with me—with us."

Sara bounced in her chair and smiled. "As much as I love being social, the fact that there's not much to do here would've had me being a hermit, trying to figure out my dissertation. I mean, the one place that serves alcohol closes at ten. There's nowhere to go dancing, and there really aren't any sports teams. Oh, and the nearest town is like an hour away. I guess I got used to Nouvelle Arniers and all it had to offer."

Anya sipped from her glass. She nodded. "I've heard that city is beautiful. Dziadzio always said it was a new city with an old soul. I wish I could visit it."

"But you can. I'll show you around. You'll love it." Sara leaned forward, her entire body bouncing. "It's such a romantic city—and I mean that in every sense of the word. They'd love your artistry. And you'd love the food, and the atmosphere. Why don't we plan a trip?"

A graceful chuckle escaped Anya's lips. She sighed. "That would be lovely, except I cannot be away from our estate beyond midnight. Papa says I'll die if I do."

Sara tilted her head. "That doesn't make any sense. Why? You sure that's not something he told you just to keep you at home? My dad said things like I couldn't date until I got married, but that wasn't literal."

Anya shrugged. "He said the medicine he gave me, that he made for me, linked me to our land in a deep way. He called it an akashic sympathy, whatever that is. He tried to explain it, but I didn't understand."

"Akashic sympathy," Sara mused. "Where have I heard that before? Anyway, and you were young, so you believed him, right?"

Anya nodded. She moved to the sofa. "He helped so many people, and he was never wrong when he made his own medicines. If there was a side effect, he prepared the person for it and gave them the choice before making it. Why would I doubt him?"

Sara nodded. "If you don't mind—and you can say no—what did he make your medicine for?"

Anya swallowed hard. "For my mind. I mean, my fear and nightmares." She paused and then sighed. Sara opened her mouth to speak, but Anya raised a hand to silence her. "Please, no. Let me tell you, but it is hard."

"No," Sara said. Concern darkening her face. "Go ahead, but only if you're sure."

Anya nodded. "Thank you. It was my second year of school and a week before my seventh birthday. Carolyn, Lida, Katja, and Rebeca chased me into the corner of the girls' shower room in the school's gymnasium. They kicked me, spat on me, and called me names. Then Carolyn made them hold me down while she poured something cold and foul-smelling from a bottle in her purse. When she lit one of those Bunsen burners from a chemistry set, I begged her to stop. I begged them to let me go. Carolyn held the fire to my face, and..."

Fear and sorrow choked Anya's voice as she spoke. Her words trailed into tears. Sara exhaled, and as her muscles relaxed, she realized she had tensed every muscle in her body. *So that's what happened.* Sara rushed to the sofa and sat beside Anya, wrapping her arms around the crying woman.

"It's okay. I mean, it's not okay what happened. But it's okay to cry. I'm here beside you."

Anya nodded. "She burned my face. That was the last day I attended school. Mama taught me until we hired a private tutor."

"I'm so sorry," Sara said. "That's horrible. You didn't deserve that. I understand now why—what are you doing?"

Sara's eyes shot wide, and her jaw dropped. Anya placed both hands on her veil. She raised it to her chin and paused. Her muscles tensed, and she sucked in a breath. Sara's heart raced at thrice the speed of the grandfather clock in the corner that thundered the seven seconds that passed in silence before Anya lifted the veil over her head. A gently curving tendril of black hair fell from Anya's severe bun, resting on her pale cheek. A long scar ran down her face from between her eyes and along the right side of her nose. The smooth, pink skin on the right side of her face had a shininess, and the brown eye on that side had no eyebrow.

Anya's jaw trembled. Their eyes met, and Sara saw fresh tears form in Anya's tear-glassed eyes. Sara smiled. Anya moved to cover her face with her hands, but Sara reached out and touched her burn-scarred cheek. Anya froze.

"The day we met," Sara said. "I tried to touch this cheek without thinking or knowing. I'm sorry. Thank you for showing me your face, but more importantly, thank you for trusting me."

Anya blushed. Her body relaxed, and she allowed her head to rest in Sara's hand. A gentle smile widened across her face. "Sara, I—you—From the moment we met, when you approached me after my performance, your smile shone through the fog and my veil. The memory of your hand's touch has stayed upon my cheek. I cannot work. I cannot read. I cannot eat without the memory of your touch and the thought of you before my mind. Whatever happens after your life returns to normal, mine is forever changed by your presence."

Sara beamed. "Then may I have permission to kiss you?"

"I...I have never kissed...anyone before, but I...yes."

Anya tensed. Sara giggled. "Relax. If you're sure, I'll lead. Okay?"

Anya nodded. Their eyes locked. Sara cupped Anya's face with her hands, brushing the toymaker's cheeks with her thumbs. Anya cooed and then bit her lower lip. Both women's chests rose and fell quickly. Sara leaned in and kissed Anya, tasting the wine on her soft lips. As she felt the warmth of Anya's breath, the scent of roses became more powerful but remained distant and dreamy.

Anya moved a tentative left hand around Sara's neck, running her fingers along the back of Sara's neck. And then her right hand moved and met the left one. Warmth filled Sara's body, and she leaned into the kiss. Her heart pounded, and butterflies flitted about her stomach.

When she broke the kiss, Sara smiled at Anya. "Well, how was your first kiss?"

Anya blinked. Her smile matched Sara's in brightness. "Could we do that again?"

Sara nodded. "Of course." And they kissed again.

Anya rubbed her right eye as she woke. She was on her side, and she never woke up on her side. Iskra wasn't in her arms either. She blinked, allowing a gasp to burst from her lips. Her breathing quickened, and her shoulders tensed. There was something warm on her back. A garbled, mumbling voice said something that almost sounded like *too early*.

Anya relaxed and nodded. A smile crept across her face as she felt Sara's arm that had been wrapped around her waist the entire time pull her closer as if she were the stuffed animal. Anya leaned into the snoring blonde, wrapping her hand around Sara's.

A few minutes, maybe half an hour, passed before realization dawned on Anya. "Today's the day. I've got to prepare."

Anya rose from the bed, and the sleeping Sara managed to string together a coherent if mumbled sentence. "No go. Stay." A chuckle escaped Anya's lips as she slipped into her black, lace-trimmed dressing gown. She leaned over and kissed Sara's cheek. "I'd love to, but I have to bake you a cake."

Anya descended to the ground floor. As she passed through the sitting room, she winced. Iskra's wooden body hung limp over the armrest of her preferred chair, a small blanket draped over her. Anya scooped the marionette into her arms and held her close.

When they reached the kitchen, Iskra shook the sleep from her own eyes and gave a dramatic yawn. She said, "Oh, it's morning. You weren't up all night reading and forgot about little old me, were you?"

Her voice lifted in both an inquisitive and teasingly accusatory way. Anya blushed. "No, I'm sorry, but I was distracted when we went to bed. I'm sorry I forgot you."

"You also forgot your veil, and we have a house guest. Is there something you want to tell me?"

Anya paused. She pressed her hand to her face and then smiled. As she walked to the cupboard to grab her baking supplies, she said, "I guess I did. Well, Sara has seen my face, so I don't need the veil until I go into town tomorrow."

Iskra spun her head to face Anya. "You what now? You showed her your face? I thought she was no different to you than anyone else."

Anya measured the dry ingredients, sifting the flour, and then placing each in a bowl. As she zested the lemons, she said, "It appears I was not being honest when I said that."

"Never would I have guessed that." Sarcasm soaked Iskra's words. "So, what did I miss? You showed her your face and then went to bed without me?"

"Let me separate the eggs," Anya said. After she had finished and discarded the shells, she washed her hands. "And then we kissed. Twice. And then we went to the bedroom."

"I knew you liked her. Anything else you want to share with your best friend?"

Anya measured the milk and then shook her head. "She's still asleep in my bed. Her snoring relaxes me, and that's it. Now, I need to focus so this is the best cake I've ever made. Do you think blueberry or strawberry to pair with the lemon?"

"I like the idea of strawberry and lemon for a cake," Sara's voice came from the kitchen doorway.

Anya and Iskra both turned and saw Sara leaning against the door frame in nothing but a black and white cotton tank top and white panties. Anya's eyes followed the curves on Sara's toned, tanned arms. She gasped as Sara sauntered toward her and planted a gentle but teasing kiss on her lips, biting Anya's lower lip as she pulled away.

"Good morning," Anya said, mixing the cake batter. "And happy birthday. I'd hoped to have this finished before you woke up, but I remained in bed longer than usual. I'll prepare breakfast and get your present once I get this in the oven."

Sara smirked and then whispered into Anya's ear. "You mean last night wasn't my present?" Anya grew flustered and splashing some of the batter on the counter. Sara giggled. "I'll make the coffee and wait for breakfast."

Sara kissed Anya's cheek and then prepared coffee for them both. Once the cake entered the oven, Sara licked the beater clean, moaning happily, while Anya whipped up a quick breakfast of porridge, spiced apples, fried potatoes, and eggs. The kitchen filled with the scents of cinnamon, clove, cardamom, ginger, apple, strawberry, and lemon.

Sara smiled and sighed contentedly. "Between the fog, the cooler weather, and these heavenly smells, it really feels like fall." She shivered. "Oh, guess I've gotten used to the humid heat of Louisiana, but this feels like home."

Anya set the plates on the table. "I'm glad you feel that way. It feels more like a home with you here than it did before you joined us. Oh! Let me get your present. I'll only be a minute."

Anya left the kitchen, returning a few minutes later with a large box wrapped in silver paper and lavender ribbon. Sara gasped when she saw its size. She tore into the wrapping paper and then opened the box. A gasp shot from her mouth before she covered it with her hands. Sara's eyes widened. Her hands trembled as she pulled the porcelain doll from inside.

"It's beautiful," she said. Her voice crept in a hushed, reverential tone. "The sculpting on this face is masterful and detailed. And...is this *me*? You sculpted a doll of me for my birthday?" Her eyes glassed with tears as she said, "Thank you."

"You are welcome." Anya smiled. "I'm glad I finished her before you decided to visit my shop."

Sara's birthday was a quiet day spent with Anya. Iskra remained largely quiet. While Sara thought Anya left her in the kitchen, when she glanced at a chair in the sitting room and later in the library, the marionette had moved to a nearby chair. Sara checked her phone at least once an hour, frowning or sighing after each check.

As the clock struck nine o'clock at night, the two women sat on the sofa in the library. Sara wrapped her arm around Anya who rested her head on Sara's chest. As she checked her phone again, Anya looked up at Sara and asked, "Is something wrong? You keep searching your phone, even though it makes you sad." Sara set her phone on the armrest. She shook her head. "I guess not. I'm sorry. It's just my friends texted me this morning before I woke up, and you've done so much for me today. I guess I figured, given the situation and all, my parents would have called or texted or something."

Anya nodded against her chest. "You mean with the money coming to them because of Mister Alexander's will? I'm sorry. It's hard not having your parents when you want to talk to them."

"It's not that I *want* to talk to her most of the time, but yeah, given that I'm the reason she's still getting that inheritance check each month. Oh well. Let's think of happier things, like my doll of a doll maker."

She leaned down and kissed Anya's soft lips, tasting the faintest hint of the citrusy tartness that remained of the lemon frosting on the cake. Their tongues brushed against each other, parting a second before their lips did. Anya's lips reached for another kiss. Sara giggled. She lifted Anya's chin with her fingers and then trailed kisses from her chin to her ear, nibbling on the lobe. A gentle moan purred from Anya's lips.

"With your permission, we could repeat last night," Sara asked.

"I would like that." Anya lifted her head and kissed Sara.

Sara turned and saw the marionette in the chair, a book open on her lap. "Sorry, Iskra, but we're heading to the bedroom. You okay?"

Iskra raised a hand and waved. "You two have fun. I'll be fine."

"How did you do that, Ani?"

Anya shrugged. "It happens."

The women rose from the sofa. Taking Sara's hand in hers, Anya led her to the large master bedroom. The lavender and yellow bedding atop the mahogany canopy bed remained unmade after Sara woke. The clothes she wore yesterday lay crumpled in a heap on the floor beside the antique armoire. Sara flipped on the light as Anya closed the door.

Anya closed the distance between them and claimed Sara's lips with her own. The warm breath from her nose tickled Sara's upper lip. Wrapping her arms around Anya's neck, Sara moaned. Her fingers slid into the toymaker's thick mass of black hair, massaging Anya's scalp. Sara's cheeks flushed as her heart quickened its pace.

"Somebody's enthusiastic," she teased.

"I am."

Anya's voice dropped a breathy octave. Warmth built in Sara's core, and she swallowed hard. Biting her lower lip, she met Anya's hungry gaze with her own. Both women's chests rose and fell in tandem.

Sara started unbuttoning Anya's mourning dress. "We're going to get you some new clothes with fewer buttons, babe." She leaned in close, allowing her lips to brush Anya's ear as she added, "I love opening a present, but this is a bit much."

"Now that I have reason to wear other clothes, perhaps I will."

As the black dress fell to the floor, the tops of Anya's full, round breasts jiggled against black and silver brocade overbust corset. Their size, along with the curve of Anya's hips and the thickness of her thighs, was an unexpected and pleasant surprise. She licked her lips.

With a swift upward motion, Sara's index finger flipped open the five clasps. The corset fell to the floor, freeing Anya's pale breasts. The toymaker arched her back and then sighed as her torso relaxed in its freedom. Sara slid behind her and cupped her breasts, kneading and massaging them. Anya gasped, arching her back and grinding her ass against Sara's crotch. A sharp, squealing gasp burst from Anya's mouth as Sara pinched her nipples.

"I love how you squirm when I touch you, Ani." Sara purred into Anya's ear as she nibbled on the toymaker's pale, slender neck. "Happy birthday to me."

7

A week passed in relative peaceful bliss. Sara and Anya spent their days apart, pursuing their own ends. Anya tended to her shop, and Sara avoided working on her dissertation by reading the books in the Skejik family library, wandering through the two massive greenhouses, and checking up on the repairs to her own house. Anything to avoid the looming deadline and the frustration of a missing source. Evenings were spent in quiet reading, conversation, and snuggling in front of the television and watching the occasional television program, usually *Jeopardy* or another game show.

Sara's phone became her wireless hotspot, as Anya had neither a computer nor Internet access in her home. Cellular and wireless Internet service proved spotty throughout most of Pazat, and as Anya had no need of such things, she never bothered to acquire them for her home or her shop. While quaint and quirky at first, the struggle of slow, unreliable Internet access plus the frustration of keeping her phone charged while it ran hot from constant use, became an annoyance.

On this chilly Thursday afternoon, a thunderstorm rumbled over a Pazat, casting an ominous shadow over the town square. The wind howled as it tore through the muddy streets, whipping debris and leaves in its wake. Dark clouds rolled overhead, turning the afternoon into a dim, gray twilight.

Thunder pealed, and lightning forked across the sky, illuminating the mountains in brief flashes of blinding light. The sound of rain was a dull but constant roar. It pounded against the roofs and streets, creating pools of water that flowed along the paths created by tire tracks in the dirt roads and through the fields. Through the lights in the buildings surrounding the town square, a traveler could see how deserted the square was, as no one ventured out of their home or business unless need dictated.

The black carriage rested just outside the back door to Skejik Toys. Anya sewed stuffed animals together in the workroom while Sara walked through the showroom snapping photographs of the store and the toys with her cell phone. She selected the seven best images and then posted them to her Instagram, Twitter, Facebook, and Hive accounts.

Just wanted to share some of the amazing handmade wooden toys and stuffed animals my girlfriend has been creating! Each piece is crafted with care and attention to detail, making them not only beautiful, but also durable and safe for little ones to play with. From cars and trains to animals and dolls, there's something for every child to enjoy. Plus, the stuffed animals are so soft and cuddly, they're sure to become a child's new best friend. If you're looking for a unique and special gift for a child in your life, be sure to check out her work either in her showroom in Pazat, PA, or in F. Schwartz and Sons' toy catalog! #handmadetoys #woodentoys #stuffedanimals #SkejikToys

Sara bounced as she walked into the workroom and sat on the chair beside Anya. She giggled. It was cute seeing Anya stick her tongue out as she focused on the precise needle strokes to embroider the detailed flowers and cats on the pale blue dress for the velveteen calico cat she had just finished making. With a goofy smile plastered on her face, Sara rested her chin in her hands and watched Anya work.

Anya winced as she pricked her ring finger. She sucked the wound and shook her hand. Out of the corner of her eye, she spotted Sara sitting there, smiling. Anya shook her head and chuckled. "There's that smile you reserve for watching artisans at work."

Sara kicked her feet in the air. "Well, I've only ever watched one master artisan, so I wasn't fully lying."

Sara reached for Anya's hand, but the toymaker wrapped her delicate pale hand around Sara's tanned fingers, pulled it to her lips, and placed a gentle kiss on its back. Her eyes smiled as they met Sara's. Sara's cheeks flushed.

"Did you get any of your work done, or have you grown bored waiting in the shop all day, dear," Anya asked.

"Nope, but I took pics of your toys to show to people, and I hit on an idea. I know you're not the biggest fan of technology and while a full website might be a bit much, but what about an Etsy store? Here." Sara opened the Etsy app on her phone. "See? All you do is make listings for your products, and if people want to buy them, they do. Then it'll send you a notice, and you ship the product to them."

Anya's eyes widened as she pored over every detail on the shop page Sara showed her. She nodded. "What if I get more orders than I can fill quickly?"

Sara's eyes widened and twinkled. Was Anya considering this? She pointed to a line on the page that told the item's estimated delivery time. "See this bit? I'm no expert, but we can set it up to give you enough time to make the doll or toy if needed and then ship it. The cool thing about sites like Etsy is people purchase knowing they're getting handmade stuff. Most people will expect you'll make the dolls after they pay for them. And you don't have to list everything—ever—but just a few things like the dolls, the plushies, and maybe some of the tin soldiers. Just a little extra money with minimal extra work."

"I could do all of this myself?" Anya tensed. "You know so much about this, but you'll go back to your life and your work. And I don't want to always ask for help. I—"

Sara squeezed Anya's hand as the toymaker's voice started trembling. "I'll be on the other side of town, Ani. I won't be that far. I'll be here for at least three years, and by then you'll be a pro at this. But if I have a reason to stay longer, who knows?"

Anya sighed. "I don't know. It's a lot to think about and plan, but I'll think about it if you think it would be a good idea."

Sara's phone rang. "Hold that thought, babe. I have to take this."

Sara walked into the showroom to take the call. Anya returned to her work, but she picked up bits of Sara's conversation as her words traveled through the cool air inside the toy shop. From initial snippets, Sara appeared to be talking to someone named Andrea from her school. The conversation started with talk of coursework and dissertation writing, and Sara tossed around four digit strings of numbers which meant nothing to Anya. But then the conversation topic shifted, piquing Anya's attention.

"Yeah, unless we have a lot more stormy days like yesterday and today," Sara said. "I should be able to move back into my house before Fall Break. Then you'll have a place to stay."

Anya sucked in a breath and held it. Her muscles tensed. She blinked twice. She swallowed hard and then released her breath. Her breathing returned in short, rapid breaths.

"I mean, there's no hotel here, not even a listing on Airbnb. Sure there's room at Ani's place, but it'd be rude to ask her to host another stranger after she let me stay there while the house gets repaired. She's great, but she is really private. Oh, you saw my post about her toys? Isn't her work amazing?" Sara giggled and brushed a wisp of blonde hair behind her left ear. "About that, yeah. I mean we haven't discussed it yet but I'm sure she feels the same way I do."

Anya blinked. How did Sara feel? Should she ask? No, that would be rude, since this is a private conversation with a friend. Just a friend. Right?

"I miss you too. I miss everyone, but I miss you the most, Andrea. If things go according to schedule, I'll be able to let you know by the end of the month. I'm so excited! Can't wait. Bye."

With a big grin on her face, Sara returned to the workroom and planted a loud kiss on Anya's cheek. Anya asked, "Nice conversation with a friend, dear?"

Sara nodded. "I miss Andrea. Moving to Pazat's been a challenge. I got so used to being able to go out and do anything at any time in Nouvelle Arniers."

Anya offered a sympathetic smile. "I've only read about that city in books, but it always did sound so exciting. Our sleepy, insular town must be dull."

Sara wrapped her arms around Anya's neck. "It's not all bad. I met you here, didn't I?"

Anya smiled and nodded. "But this Andrea who is coming to see you, who is she?"

Sara laughed. "Are you jealous?"

"No." Anya shook her head. "I am only curious."

Sara rested her head on Anya's shoulder. "I mean, sure she's tall and gorgeous with lustrous black hair, brown eyes, and a great rack. She's also brilliant and compassionate. Who wouldn't fall for that? But she's married and not interested in women at all." Her tone shifted from teasing to serious. "Besides, if I'm going to have a girlfriend, I only want one. And I'd like you to be her."

"Girlfriend." The word slipped through Anya's mouth in hushed tones. Her voice's volume slowly rose, and a smile spread across her face. "Girlfriend. Me? Girlfriend. I like—I would like that. Yes."

They kissed. When the kiss ended, Sara said, "Then it's settled. We'll get you a computer, set up your Etsy page, and make us Facebook official. Oh, and don't worry about the showroom. I'll sweep and lock up, so we can get home earlier. Love you."

As Sara walked into the showroom, Anya smiled. "Love you too."

Nestled one block south from Pazat's town square, sat the town's only bookstore, Bookworm's Delight. This two-story building had the owner's home on the second floor, and the owners Franz and Paula Koranov, took pride in making their shop feel like an extension of their home. A cheerful shade of canary yellow covered the store's wooden exterior, and large, square windows displayed an array of books and trinkets. A colorful array of blue, yellow, and purple flowers sat in both windowsills, and on the sill to the right of the entrance, a plump yellow cat, Taran, slept atop a pile of books he had knocked over when searching for the perfect bit of sunlight in which to nap. In addition to its wide selection of books and magazines, the bookstore also offered a variety of other products such as bookmarks, pens, journals, and book-themed gifts. Beside the counter is a chalkboard sign with hand drawn images and lettering announcing the upcoming events at the bookstore, the monthly blook club meeting, a poetry reading by Penn State creative writing graduate students, and a tea party.

The aroma of book leather, paper, and freshly brewed coffee filled the interior. The coffee's warmth contrasted with the cool, crisp air inside, caused by the owners leaving small cracks in the store's windows. Tall oak bookshelves line the walls and fill most of the floor, each shelf carefully curated by the owner and staff. As with most bookstores, the books are organized by genre, with books of local interest being the first category visitors see upon entry. Off to the left, behind a half wall, was the children's section filled with age-appropriate books, a selection of toys both from Skejik Toys and national brands, and a play mat. Situated in the rear of the store was a cozy reading nook, complete with comfortable armchairs, seasonal scented candles, and a fireplace. Beside the reading nook was a small coffee shop, selling a humble assortment of coffees and teas, and on the weekends, Paula Koranov added pastries, cookies, and candies to the menu.

Saturdays tended to be busy days, and today was no different. Half of the town crowded into the bookstore for pastries, coffee, and the occasional book purchase. Taran milled about the store, alternating between finding a quiet spot to nap and begging food and attention from the patrons, which he always received. Franz Koranov stood behind the register. His fluffy mop of white hair, thick mustache, and round spectacles that slid along the ridge of his bulbous nose led many children to call him Geppetto. He greeted customers as they entered, chatted with them as they checked out, and radiated joy and friendliness.

In the middle of the afternoon, the bookstore's foot traffic slowed, allowing Franz Koranov to walk to the coffee shop and pour himself a cup of strong coffee with two sugars and a teaspoon of cream. After he returned to his post at the register, Taran meowed from the center of the store as the door opened. Sara held the door as Anya entered the store before following her inside and entwining her finger with those of the toymaker. Franz Koranov turned toward the open door, blinked twice in surprise, and said, "Afternoon, Sara. How are you and...Miss Skejik today?"

His voice suggested an unexpected level of surprise. Anya said, "I'm well, Mister Koranov. How are you?"

Sara beamed. "I'm doing okay too, Sir. Busy day?"

"She speaks?" Franz Koranov muttered the question under his breath. Upon the realization that he spoke that thought aloud, he gasped. "Sorry, I—uh—is it just the two of you?"

Sara giggled and squeezed Anya's hand. "Who else would be with us?"

The shop owner ran his chubby fingers through his hair and said with a sheepish grin, "Well, Miss Skejik never visits us without her little friend Iskra, so I was taken aback."

Anya nodded. "She wished to remain at home while we shopped."

"Oh, of course." He nodded quickly. "Anything I can help you ladies with?"

"I need something to teach me about computers and websites," Anya said.

"But first, we're going to have coffee and see if Mrs. Koranov baked any of those kolaczkis like she did last week."

He smiled and nodded. "She made three varieties this weekend, apple, fig, and cranberry. There were a handful of each when I walked back for some coffee a few minutes ago."

With its proximity to the reading nook, the coffee shop had only a handful of small tables and armchairs for guests to use. The pillar candles atop the tables and the pastry case perfumed the air with the scent of spiced apples. A few customers sat in the coffee shop, drinking and reading while enjoying a quiet respite from their day. They eyed the two women curiously. Hushed whispers and silent text messages were exchanged regarding Anya Skejik holding Sara Alexander's hand without holding Iskra in her arm.

Black flecks peppered Paula Koranov's silver bob. Wrinkles creased her round face, rippling out from her gentle smile and around her wide, deep set brown eyes. The gentle flickering of a candle flame reflected in her half-moon glasses. She wore her rosary around her neck and covered her clothes in a white apron with red and gold embroidery.

The two women ordered and then sat at one of the few two-person tables remaining empty. Anya's coffee was black, but Sara preferred cream, two spoonfuls of sugar, and a bit of hazelnut syrup in hers. The coffee came in Bookworm's Delight branded mugs, and each woman had a small plate with two of each of the three kolaczki varieties. As the sumptuous, rich, sweetness of the fig jam-filled cookie ignited Sara's taste buds, she bounced in her seat and kicked her legs against those of the chair.

"Hey, Ani, why is everyone so formal with you? You're always *Miss Skejik*." Sara leaned close and smirked. Her voice lowered to a dramatic whisper. "You're not a thousand-year-old vampire, are you?"

Anya responded with a single, slow blink. She chuckled and shook her head. "I don't believe such things exist outside of fiction, but I don't know why. It's always been that way since I took over the family toy shop. I'll be thirty in January, but that doesn't explain why the older people treat me as an elder."

"I didn't realize you were almost two years older than me. When I first moved here, everyone talked about you like you've just always been an adult. It was weird."

Anya sipped her coffee. "Do you think I'll be able to have an online store and keep up by myself?"

"Having second thoughts?" Sara leaned forward and scanned Anya's face through her veil.

"I'm just nervous. That computer and that Etsy site, there was so much to learn and so many forms with the bank, and then you want me to have an Instagram and a Hive but not a Twitter. It's just a lot."

Sara nodded. They walked to the bookstore to take a break from setting everything up at the shop. Anya had a panic attack when strangers started interacting with her Instagram posts. She reached out and wrapped her hands around Anya's coffee-warmed hands. A faint smile was visible through the toymaker's veil. Sara beamed.

"It's okay. You'll get it. Look, in all likelihood, you might get two or three sales the first month or so. That's why we set your ship time to three weeks after the order. It gives you time to do the amazing work you do. And other than next weekend, I'll be with you every step of the way in getting used to it, but I'll be back the following Monday."

Anya stiffened. "Next weekend? Where will you go?"

"Oh!" Sara giggled and playfully slapped her head. "I forgot to tell you. I'll be in New York, searching the Ottendorfer, Academy of Medicine, and the Public Libraries for my dissertation. Hey! I know what you're going to say, but why don't you come with me? It'll be a nice vacation. We can stay at a romantic hotel, just the two of us?"

Sara's index finger traced hearts on the back of Anya's hand. She held her breath. Her muscles tensed as the toymaker's seemed to relax. Anya's eyes closed, and her head lowered. She swallowed hard. The scent of roses pierced through the spiced apple scent from the candles. Stronger but still distant and dreamlike.

Before Anya could respond, Sara sighed a deep and mournful sigh. She nodded. "It's okay, Ani. I know. We're just different people." She chuckled darkly. "Opposites do attract. Well, let's enjoy our time together."

Sunday morning was cool and dry with only a light haze hanging in the air. Anya left earlier than usual, as she wanted to work on her first Etsy order before opening the the shop. Sara kissed her goodbye and promised to have supper ready when she returned. Once Anya and Iskra were no longer in view of the front door, Sara locked the door, set an alarm on her cell phone, and then walked up to the bedroom she shared with Anya and took two bobby pins from Anya's vanity.

Sara descended the stairs and made her way to the locked door that led to the tower where Dr. Boris Skejik treated patients. The music room once served as a waiting area for his patients, but now dust blanketed the chaise lounges, chairs, the grand piano, harp, and viola. Memories of both sorrow and joy hung in the cool air.

The door to the office had a bronze sign that read *Dr. Boris P. Skejik, Physician*. Having seen this done countless times on television and in movies, Sara twisted and pulled the bobby pins into makeshift lock picks. She took a deep breath and exhaled slowly.

"Okay, I can do this," she said aloud to herself. "All I have to do is slide these in the lock and jiggle them around until it opens. Easy. Just hope I don't get caught. That was Anya's one rule for me staying here."

Sara slid the bobby pins into the lock and pushed them in and out. A few clicks and bumps later, she heard a snap. The pins broke. She fished the snapped bit out of the lock, grumbled, and then walked back upstairs to retrieve two more bobby pins. "If this doesn't work, then I'll steal the key from Anya's keyring. There has to be something in here like a file on her condition. Something that would have her dad make that bogus claim about a curse." She looked up a lock picking video on YouTube. "Okay, so I have to jiggle and listen for clicking noises. I'll be more gentle."

Sara attempted to pick the lock again. The tip of her tongue slipped between her lips as she focused. Slowing her pace, she pressed her ear against the door and listened. With only a vague understanding of the sound she needed to hear, Sara pushed and pulled the pins, feeling the resistance of the tumblers. One slid and clicked. Then the second and third tumbler clicked into place. She opened the door.

Sara opened her mouth, smiling, and bounced. "I did it. It worked! Oh this would have been so helpful to know how to do when I locked myself out of my dorm room in undergrad."

The smell of dust and old chemicals floated from the old doctor's office. Sara's nose twitched. She switched on the light in the office, and the surveyed the room that had once been the town doctor's office.

The small, hexagonal room had heavy blue curtains covering tall rectangular windows. Dust covered everything, including the stairs leading up to the second floor and down to the basement. A handmade varnished oak desk and a filing cabinet sat against one of the windows. A ceramic mug filled with pens and pencils, an old black physician's bag, a gray typewriter, and a leather journal sat atop the desk. A bookshelf with a series of leather journals identical to the one on the desk, an examination table, a sink, and a cabinet—presumably for medical supplies—were also present.

Scrunching her face and letting her tongue protrude from her pursed lips, Sara opened the filing cabinet and searched. No medical records filled the cabinet, only invoices and other business financial documents. Sara shrugged. "I guess we'll try the journal on the desk."

Sara sat in the oak swivel chair and flipped through the journal. It wasn't a case record, but it was Boris Skejik's personal journal. The doctor's handwriting was crisp and precise but filled with flourishes that Sara had only seen in Victorian or Edwardian correspondence. Most of the entries were dull and tedious, describing his day down to the precise number of grams of porridge he ate at breakfast and the number of strawberries he had for an afternoon snack. Sara yawned, but she continued scanning his journal.

She paid more attention when the entries mentioned Anya. Sara smiled. Apparently, Anya was a friendly child who loved physical affection, especially hugs, before things changed. Sara winced as guilt stabbed her. This was private information, and she promised she wouldn't disturb Anya's father's office. But she had to know where this ignorant idea of a curse came from. When she reached the entries right after Anya was burned by her classmates, Sara's stomach churned. Her father described the burns in detail, the color of the puss, and the pain as Anya described it. He described her nightmares, trembles, and flashbacks when the hearth fires were lit. With painstaking detail, Boris Skejik chronicled his daughter's shift from happy, outgoing child to a terrified introvert who refused to talk to anyone other than her family, the servants, and her tutor. And then she found the entry she needed.

Today I must make a confession that weighs heavily on my conscience. My dearest daughter Dobrianya, whom I love more than anything in the world, has been suffering from severe anxiety for some time now as a result of her loneliness after we pulled her from the school for her own safety. In my desperation to help her, I turned to my alchemical studies and created the Tincturam Magnae Animae to treat her condition.

Three months have passed, and she has received daily injections. Unfortunately, the results have been disastrous. Not only has her anxiety refused to be quelled, but the medicine has made her bodily fluids toxic. Her saliva shows traces of the snakeroot and belladonna, and when fed to the rats in my laboratory, they died within hours.

I fear for her health and safety. She secretes the dreamy scent of the Vysnívaná ruža at all times, and when she is anxious or excited, the scent is stronger, impacting the psyches of those around her with greater intensity and for longer durations. Those who have an allergy to its scent grow angry in her presence, and I fear she may interpret this as them being angry at her for something she has done.

In a moment of weakness, I invented a lie to protect her. I told her the tincture has the side effect of placing her in a sympathetic bond with our family's land and that if she were to leave our family land for more than twenty-four hours, like an unwatered rose, she would wither and die.

I know this is wrong, and I cannot shake off the guilt that consumes me. I hide this from her and my beloved Lana. I cannot bear the thought of causing harm to my own child. I have failed as a father and as an alchemist. I must find a way to make things right, to find a cure for my daughter and to ease her suffering.

I hope that one day I will be able to confess the truth to her and make amends for my mistake. Until then, I will continue to pray for her health and well-being.

Sara sank in the wooden chair and exhaled. She ran her fingers through her hair. Her head nodded as she sat in silence. Sara exhaled again. She said, "Well, at least the toxicity of her bodily fluids has gone away, but I guess getting the medicine out of her system for years will do that."

Sara paused. Her tongue pushed against her right cheek, and her gaze rose toward the ceiling. She blinked. "Wait! Did I read that correctly?"

She read the entry again and then whistled. "Fuck, the medicine Ani's dad gave her was the *Tincturam Magnae Animae*! He used it for her mental illness, which is in line with how I understand Hahnemann's homeopathic thesis' application. Did he adapt it properly? It should have worked if he did."

Sara searched the late physician's journal at a frantic pace. If Boris Skejik made the *Tincturam*, then he obviously knew about Paracelsus' *De Mirabilibus Occultis Naturae*. Did he own a copy? No, that book is too rare for a small-town doctor, but maybe he came across it in medical school.

Rifling through the pages of the journal, Sara found the steps taken in producing the *Tincturam*. It could be replicated. Sara's breathing quickened. No, it could be perfected, which meant if she could discern his mistakes, Sara could recreate the medicine given to Anya without the nasty side effects.

Sara paused. Her heart pounded against her chest. What brought on that idea? Love? Sara shrugged. Maybe, but she was a historian and not a scientist. But she had the steps, and if this was Boris Skejik's office, his laboratory must be in the house as well. That's where the information she needed would be.

Sara's face lit up. Holding the journal to her chest, she bounced. "I can complete my dissertation. I've found a link. If only Dr. Skejik were still alive to fill in the gaps. Damn. Now how do I get—"

The alarm on Sara's phone cut her off. She froze. Anya would be home in half an hour. Sara returned the journal to the desk and left the physician's office, closing the door behind her.

While Sara searched for information in Boris Skejik's former medical office, Carolyn Ward sat in her sitting room, enjoying a glass of Chardonnay while reading her Bible. The high ceilings adorned with elegant crown molding added depth to the already spacious room. The tall windows lining the walls filled the room with the gentle warmth of natural light. A plush, burgundy and gold Turkish rug adorned the hardwood floor, its golden tassels extending from Carolyn's mahogany and burgundy corduroy armchair to the white marble fireplace and mantle, lined with family photographs and an urn. She had the fireplace installed after her husband's death, replacing the rough stone hearth and wooden mantle that had previously sat against the northern wall. A flat screen television hung from the wall over the mantle.

As she closed the white leather Bible, Paul Petska, her ranch supervisor, knocked on the archway before entering. He was a tall man with a small beer belly. His olive skin had darkened and leathered with the many decades spent in the field. A green John Deere hat hid the receding line of his curly black hair. When Carolyn nodded to him, he removed his hat, smoothed his hair, and nodded.

"Good afternoon, Mrs. Ward." His voice was deep and haggard. Decades of drinking and smoking had taken their toll. "I just came to alert you we may have to destroy the last few batches of milk and some of the cows we've butchered."

Carolyn sighed. Her eyes narrowed in annoyance. "And why is that? This is our most lucrative season. Why are we destroying profit?"

Paul rubbed the back of his neck with his meaty right hand. "Turns out there's some snakeroot in the grazing fields, and at least a couple of the cows were seen eating it."

"Will this affect the flavor?"

Carolyn was impatient. He knew that. Paul shook his head. "No, ma'am. It's poisonous. The cows can eat it, sure, but it gets into the milk and goes to humans who drink it. Makes them real sick. It's like food poisoning, and if they're not careful, it can kill them. Just wanted to let you know, so we can avoid any trouble."

"You will do nothing, Paul. Nothing."

"But, Mrs. Ward, we don't want to hurt anyone. We can get a USDA team out here to test the milk and meat, but that'll take time."

"And money, and we won't be doing that. I haven't turned my dear late husband's farm from a comfortable living to a profitable and luxurious home. If it makes you feel better, I will pray that no one is hurt."

The old farm worker shrugged. He sighed. This would be a futile fight. "I'll do that too. But can I at least uproot and burn the damn thing."

"Wait a week before deciding. If no one gets hurt, then don't do anything. I think this will be you worrying over nothing. And Paul, there's not need to tell your sister about this. It'll just make her more anxious."

"Yes, ma'am. Thank you, ma'am." Paul Petska nodded heavily, turned, and left the house.

8

The next few days passed in solitude's silence for Sara. Anya had received half a dozen special orders from the Esty store, and feeling obligated to complete them as quickly as possible, she spent longer hours in her workroom.

Sara spent much of her free time searching Boris Skejik's former office for more information regarding what he knew of Paracelsus' *De Mirabilibus Occultis Naturae*. She found his operating room and his laboratory. The stench of rat droppings stank up the stale air in the lab. Books and journals filled with alchemical and pharmaceutical knowledge and formulae and gnawed on by rats filled the lab's bookcase, and partially empty vials, syringes, and jars of chemicals unused for years littered the work table. The book she sought was not there. She did however, find another journal detailing his quest to cure her, and she found herself captivated by one entry enough to read through it a dozen times.

I find myself in a state of great turmoil as I contemplate my decision to use the tincturam magnae to cure Dobrianya's growing anxiety and fear of social interaction. Her nightmares have grown in both frequency and intensity, and she has ceased communicating with anyone but her mother and I without speaking through the marionette Iskra. I have always prided myself on my knowledge and expertise, but in this moment, I am plagued by doubt and uncertainty.

On the one hand, I know that my daughter's anxiety and trauma have been constant sources of suffering for her, and that traditional treatments have been ineffective. From the theorizing of both Agrippa and Parcelsus and the application of Hahnemann's homeopathic thesis, I have created this tincture that by all accounts should provide her with the relief she so desperately needs.

On the other hand, I am well aware of the risks involved in using an untested treatment on a human subject. There are several plants with toxic properties used in the tincture's creation, and the soil here does not have the proper nutrients needed to grow the proper strain of roses, thus making my own hybrid breed mere approximations of what I should be using. I could have imported a strain from Kyiv had I thought it would be of necessity, but I fear waiting any longer will make her condition incurable. I only hope this tincture will have minimal unintended side effects; although it could prove to be fatal. The thought of causing harm to my own child is unbearable.

I have spent countless hours in my laboratory, pouring over books and conducting experiments on rats in the hope of finding a cure for my daughter's condition. But now, as the moment of truth approaches, I find myself filled with a sense of dread and foreboding.

I am torn between my love for Dobrianya and my duty as a responsible physician. I do not know what the right decision is, and the weight of this choice is heavy upon my shoulders.

I can only pray that whatever path I choose, it will be the one that leads to my daughter's healing and happiness.

How could she tell Anya what she found? How do you tell your girlfriend her father had knowingly poisoned her and made up that story about a curse to cover his own ass? And how to you tell her you violated her trust for selfish reasons and learned all this in the process? While this wouldn't be a happily ever after given their differences broken trust was not how Sara wanted the relationship to end.

On this Wednesday evening, as the sun dipped below the peaks of the Pocono Mountains, Sara packed her blue and white striped suitcase for her trip to New York City. As the *Rainbow of History* podcast played in the background, she folded her purple and black flannel shirt and placed it atop her jeans. She hugged the porcelain doll Anya made her for her birthday. A wistful smile spread across her face. Sara smiled, and then she sighed.

Setting the doll in her suitcase but not taking her hand away, she paused. *What if someone steals her while I'm not in my hotel room? It's a silly fear, but it happens. I've heard stories from friends who had things stolen, and I found that subreddit where hotel workers confessed stealing things. But I just want something to remind me of her when I'm gone—while I'm gone.*

She picked the doll up and hugged her once more, letting the hug linger for a minute before setting the doll atop the pillows. "Maybe I'll ask for one of the blouses she wears under her dresses, something that smells like her," she said. After a sigh, Sara added, "Why are you getting this sentimental? You're going to be ending this within three years. She's not going to change her weird, introverted ways. Doesn't matter that she's so kind, gentle, and caring—or that I feel more at home around her than I have in years. She's an uneducated, small-town girl who has no desire to leave her home. I'm an academic. I go where the jobs are. Shouldn't have gotten attached. We're from different worlds."

Sara zipped her suitcase. She loosed a trio of dark chuckles. "Yeah, this time *I* said it. I knew it coming in. This isn't some stupid heterosexual Hallmark holiday movie where a big city lawyer goes to a small town where her family lived, finds a hot farmhand who teaches her to enjoy the slow pace of life there, carve pumpkins, and abandon her life to open a chocolate shop. Start acting like life works that way, and you get your heart broken."

Sara sat on the bed and cuddled an old stuffed bear with mismatched button eyes. She was back in the spring semester of her sophomore year of college, and Amy Ferguson, the pitcher for the Lady Cats softball team. Things had been going well, and then word came that Amy was going to be invited to try out for the US Olympic team. As the tryouts neared, Amy spent more and more time practicing and working out at the gym. Date night restaurants changed to those supporting healthy foods, but date nights occurred at a reduced frequency. Sara convinced herself that attending the games Amy coached when not playing herself to be their dates.

The time alone got to Sara, and she complained that she felt forgotten. That started a fight. Amy ended the fight by saying, "It's been fun, but we're from different worlds. You live in the library, and I live in the stadium. Thanks for the memories."

Sara wiped away the tears that formed in her eyes. That was over eight years and a dozen girlfriends ago, but she still felt the hurt when memories surfaced. Time was a slow healer. Maybe one day the pain would dull enough to not notice, but to day was not that day.

Three soft knocks sounded on the door. Sara shook herself back to the present and asked, "Yes?"

The door opened a sliver, revealing the side of Anya's face. "May I enter?"

"Of course." Sara smiled. As Anya, holding Iskra, stepped into the bedroom, they hugged. Anya kissed Sara's cheek, and Sara said, "It's your old room, Ani, and it's your house. You can come in."

Anya nodded, tiredness visible on her smiling face. "But I have given you this space as your own. Politeness and respect dictate knocking before entering."

"You need to explain that to my mother." Sara snorted. "Wait, better yet, let's not put you through that just yet. Busy day?"

Anya nodded. "I should have all of the new orders ready to ship by Sunday, assuming tomorrow is a quieter day than today was."

"Yeah? A lot of people came by?"

Before Anya could respond, Iskra draped herself over Anya's arm, falling limp, sighing, and saying, "We had twelve people come to buy toys. It was like they never stopped coming, but..." The marionette paused and sat up dramatically. "Anya here talked to three adults all by herself. Freaked them out by doing it. I was so proud."

Sara blinked. "Oh? Should I be worried about you talking to people who aren't me?"

Anya blushed. She shook her head. "No." Her gaze drifted to the suitcase atop the bed for a moment. Her voice stiffened as she said, "Have you finished packing?"

Sara offered a tentative nod. "Everything I can pack before tomorrow morning. I'll be back on Sunday evening." She took hold of Anya's hand, squeezed it, and added, "Unless you want to come—no, you've got your orders to fill. And I have my research."

Anya nodded, her gaze lowered toward the floor. Sara's stomach turned over and then growled in anger. Anya said, "I've made supper, so if you're as hungry as your stomach says, you should come eat."

Sheepishly, Sara nodded. "Seems I forgot to eat today. Supper sounds nice."

The weekend drug its heels into the soil as it trudged onward. While Sara searched the libraries of New York City for the legendary and rare Paracelsus text, Anya and Iskra toiled at the toy store. Anya returned to her habit of leaving home at dawn and remaining at the store until sunset, walking home by the last remnants of the day's light. She fixed herself a quick and simple supper, selected a book from the library, and sat beside one of the front windows, constantly peering into the foggy darkness before settling into her large bed alone.

As the Sunday sun set, Anya finished the last of the Etsy orders. Upon returning home, she sent the carriage to Sara's house, knowing Sara's car wouldn't be able to drive around the debris along the pathway. Maybe that would change in the near future. Anya ate a bowl of cold porridge for supper and resumed her reading by the window.

After the seventh peek into the night's deepening darkness, Iskra reached a wooden hand up and poked Anya's chin. "She'll be home soon. Remember, she called half an hour ago from Binghamton. She'll be here before nine o'clock."

"I know." Anya said. "I just—It's been lonely and quiet these past few days, and I..."

Iskra filled the pause by saying, "You miss her."

Anya nodded. "I don't understand it. Aside from you, I've lived alone for fourteen years and have always been fine."

"No, you haven't."

"Yes, I have." Anya straightened herself in the chair.

Iskra shook her head. "There's a difference in growing accustomed to something and being fine."

Anya shook her head and returned to her book. The night continued with her reading in silence, pausing every few minutes to check the window. The grandfather clock chimed once on the half hour, and Sara had not yet returned. Anya's heart thumped quickly in her chest. The clock chimed for nine o'clock. She sighed. She peeked through the curtain at a greater frequency.

Sara hadn't returned. Anya closed her book with a heavy sigh. She peered through the window glass into the night beyond once more before rising from her chair, Iskra clutched in one arm like a stuffed animal and her book held by the hand of the other. After returning the book to its place on one of the shelves in the library, she cast a forlorn gaze at the locked front door. Anya lowered her head and then began her ascent.

The lock clicked, and the door opened. Anya's breath and her steps halted. A long, drawn-out yawn preceded Sara's entrance into the foyer. Anya released her breath, and Iskra yelped as she fell to the stairs. Anya raced to the door where she and Sara embraced each other in a long, deep hug. As they pulled back from the embrace, their lips met in tender, lingering kiss.

"Welcome home," Anya said. A smile broadened across her face as her shoulders relaxed from a tension she didn't realize she carried.

Sara took a deep breath as she returned the smile. "I missed you too, Ani."

Sara closed and locked the door. Anya grabbed Sara's suitcase. "How was your trip? Did you take any photographs? What were the libraries like? Did you find the book you need? Tell me everything."

"In the morning, babe," Sara said through smirking lips and a twinkling smile. Her voice dropped half an octave. "But first, I need to feel your skin against mine."

"Yeah, yeah, yeah," Iskra said. "I'll sleep in the sitting room."

Anya held out her hand, palm up, and asked, "Shall we then?"

Sara took her hand and nodded. "Yes."

Morning came too early. Anya woke before dawn, as was her habit, but smiled as she rolled over, draping her arm around the snoring blonde beside her. Curled in a fetal position, a contented, cooing sigh interrupted the snoring. Sara wrapped her arms around Anya's and pulled her closer.

Anya chuckled. "I can spare a few moments, my darling. At least until the dawn breaks."

Dawn brought gentle sunshine that slipped in through the windows. Anya slipped her arm free of Sara's grasp and then kissed her girlfriend's cheek, whispering a declaration of love into her ear, and then left the bed. She dressed, scooped up Iskra from the den, and headed to the kitchen to fix herself breakfast. The rich scent of steeping coffee filled the kitchen. The shredded potatoes sizzled in the cast iron skillet while Anya scrambled four eggs.

As she sliced two tomatoes, Sara slipped into the kitchen, yawned, and said, "Didn't think you'd be that hungry after last night."

Anya smiled and flipped the potatoes. She sprinkled salt and pepper on the tomato slices. "I thought you might be hungry when you woke up, dear. I'm glad your breakfast won't be cold."

Sara poured and prepared two cups of coffee, yawning as she stirred the milk into hers. "Yeah, well, I thought I'd join you in the shop today."

Anya smiled as she grilled the tomatoes. "Mondays are usually slow, so having company will be nice. And you call tell me all about your trip. I've always wanted to visit New York City's libraries, museums, and zoos. I've never seen a zoo. Did you go to a zoo?"

Sara sipped her coffee and then yawned. "I need to get my run in, after we get to the shop. Might pop by the diner while out and get another round of coffee. But no, I didn't hit any of the zoos. Too bad, the Bronx Zoo just announced viewing was available for some fennec fox cubs and snow leopard kittens. All those big ears and floofy tails would have been so cute to see, but no, I spent most of my time being led around massive libraries only to be told they had nothing to help me. Rare and possibly no longer existent alchemical manuscripts are hard to find."

"I'm sorry," Anya said as she sat at the small kitchen table. "I had hoped this trip would give you what you needed. I know it's not the same thing as medical school, but Papa told stories about how difficult and stressful that was."

Through a mouth filled with fried potatoes, Sara responded, saying, "Yeah, but if I screw up, no one dies, at least. Oh, I got a call from the contractor this morning. That's what woke me up. Seems the repairs will be ready tomorrow afternoon. I'll have to go back home."

Anya nodded, offering a faint smile. "That is...good. I knew the day would come, but I had hoped it would be a while longer. I will miss having you here."

Sara smiled and sipped her coffee. "I'll miss you too, but I'll come visit often. And I'm sure I can spend the night once or twice a week. We'll still be together, just not living together. Oh! I've been meaning to ask, is it true your father was an alchemist? I've heard a few people around town say that, so that's the only reason I ask."

Anya pursed her lips and pushed her eggs around on her plate. Iskra stiffened in her chair. Anya closed her eyes and said, "He always called himself a physician and an herbalist. He made medicines from his books when we couldn't get shipments in or when someone couldn't afford the big pharmacy company's medicine."

"And didn't he make your medicine? I'm sorry, but I've heard stories. And if what I've heard was true, he might have the book I need or might have a name of someone who would."

Sara's words were hesitant but gilded with a hopefulness and excitement. She sucked in a breath, tensing her muscles to hold it as she waited for an answer. Anya cut and chewed her grilled tomato. Her eyes remained closed. Sara swallowed hard. Her heart pounded in her throat. Did she push too far?

Anya scooped a bite of the scrambled eggs onto her fork and ate it. She chewed the bite thoroughly, her eyes closed and her head lowered, before offering a response in a shaking whisper. "Nothing had worked. Mama and Dziadzio agreed with him. I tried pill after pill, but nothing made me feel better." She paused and rubbed her upper arm. "Papa gave me injections daily for six months, but they didn't help. People got mad at me more often. And then I lost Mama and Papa."

Anya teared up, choking her voice. Her hands shook. She dropped the fork and knife she was holding and pushed away from the table. Sara leaped from her seat and wrapped Anya in her arms. The toymaker broke down and sobbed, her salty tears soaking Sara's burgundy sweater. Iskra sat, her head bowed but nodding.

"The policeman said it was an accident. I wasn't near them. I was with Dziadziu at the shop. But people talked. They said

I did it. They said Papa ignored them to focus on his freak daughter. They shouted and threw things at me. I guess the curse affected them too."

That damned "curse." Sara clenched her jaw to avoid saying what she wanted to say. Curses aren't real. But Anya had just opened up about her parents' death. Now wasn't the time.

"I'm so sorry, baby," Sara said. "It wasn't your fault. Please don't blame yourself. It makes sense to lock off his old office and lab."

Anya nodded, her face buried in Sara's shoulder. Through her tears, Anya said, "There are other reasons, but yes. I'm sorry, but I can't go in there again. I can't look. I..." Her voice broke. "I just wish I could leave this town."

But you can, Ani. You can leave this little town. If I could shake your eyes open and get you to look away from the past, we could be so happy together. But you're stuck. I knew it before I left Nouvelle Arniers. Everyone in this little town is stuck in the mindset of never leaving their hometown. It was my fault for trying.

After a quiet Monday, Sara slept in on Tuesday. Travel fatigue caught up with her, and she woke just before lunch. Sara bathed quickly, ate a light lunch, and dressed. She checked the house, and upon ensuring she was alone, Sara slipped once more into the office and laboratory of Doctor Boris Skejik.

The office hadn't changed since the last searched it, save for a reduction in the stale stench of the air. Sara's hand traced the edge of the late doctor's diary, but she chose to leave it unopened this time. Focusing her attention on his desk drawers, Sara found office supplies, a handful of empty Charleston Chew wrappers, a small animal skeleton, a dozen pictures of Anya as a child, and a note from Anya's mother saying she knew about the candy stash. Apparently, the doctor wasn't as diligent at managing his diabetes as he instructed patients to be.

Sara chuckled. That sounded like her dad and his twelve Sprites a day habit. She pulled a handle on the desk, opening a small writing surface. A clang drew her attention. An old straight razor with a rusted blade that had a reddish brown stain on the edge had fallen to the floor. Strange place for a razor. Was there a mirror as well?

Sara kneeled and searched, but found no mirror. She lifted her gaze to the underside of the writing surface. A folded piece of paper from a spiral notebook, the rough edges dangling unevenly, protruded from the desk. Sara shrugged and grabbed the paper. The handwriting was neat and feminine, adorned with flourishes and little angled hearts in place of the dots atop the i's. Sara started reading.

I am so sorry, Papa. It's been so hard with you and Mama gone. Dziadzio tries, but he's getting old. He can't play with me as much as you could. He spends all day in his shop, leaving me here with Iskra. He doesn't believe me when I say she talks to me and she moves, but it's true. Why won't anyone listen? When he comes home, he yells at me to take my medicine, but the pills we get from the doctor in Honesdale make me worse. He doesn't understand. The nightmares are worse. I'm surrounded by fire and smoke and laughter. I run through the flames, calling for you. I hear you. I hear Mama. But you aren't there. Neither is she. I even hear Iskra, but I can't find her either. The fire laughs as it grows, surrounding me, dancing near me. It burns again and again and again.

I shouldn't have done it, Papa, but I can't take it. My tummy hurts, and I feel sick when I eat. I'm sad all the time, and everyone hates me. They say I smell weird, and it makes them mad. I tried to follow your notes and make the special medicine you made for me, but I did something wrong. I don't know what I did, but it burns when I put the needle in my arm. And then I get dizzy and pass out. I should have listened to the priest and burned your books when you and Mama had your accident.

Sara gasped. Her gaze turned to the razor on the floor, and then it returned to the note in her hand. She swallowed hard.

After a deep sigh, through a shaky whispered voice, Sara asked, "Is this why she locked the office?"

Sara folded the note and placed it in the back pocket of her jeans. She searched through the remaining desk drawers but found nothing of interest. Drawer by drawer, the filing cabinet offered no more than unfulfilled promises. But in the back of the otherwise empty bottom drawer, Sara found a small notepad. The first page was blank, but the second page was titled *Books To Burn Upon My Death*. The first few books listed were occult books, Bacon's *De Nigromancia*, *Le Dragon Noir*, the infamous Red Book, and the *Lemegeton*.

"What were you into, doc?" Sara shook her head. "Even in New Orleans, these books aren't easy to find, and you'd still get a lot of subtle looks." She turned the next page, and her eyes widened. "Oh, what's this? Agrippa? Seems I've found the alchemists."

Sara had found the list of alchemical texts Boris Skejik owned. Aside from Agrippa, she noticed familiar and expected names such as Albertus Magnus, John Dee, Gilles de Rais, and Johannes Trithemius. Where was Paracelsus? Had she missed him? No alchemist's library was complete without at least a copy of *Das Buch Paragranum*.

Sara searched the list again, and she had indeed missed the multiple entries for works by Paracelsus. Her heart pounded, but her breath stopped. Through tensed muscles, Sara read through entries, beginning with the medical books and then into the alchemical texts. There, after *Ex Libro de Nymphis, Sylvanis, Pygmaeis, Salamandris et Gigantibus, etc.*, was *De Mirabilibus Occultis Naturae*.

"She knew. No, did she? She knew he had books, but did she know he had *that* book?" Sara turned her gaze to the bookshelf and pushed her tongue into her cheek as she scanned the shelf once more. Sara shook her head. "I searched that shelf already, and I didn't see it. Guess I'll look somewhere else."

Taking the notepad with her, Sara ascended the stairs to the laboratory where Boris Skejik prepared the medicines and alchemical concoctions he used in his practice. Shelves with small amber glass bottles containing long dried herbs, pharmaceutical powders, and the gritty and dried remains of various medicinal syrups lined the interior walls. Scientific and alchemical equipment such as scales, Bunsen burners, an alembic, a crucible, an athanor, and multiple mortars and pestles sat atop atop the desk and table along with a handful of books, all blanketed by a thick layer of dust. Papers stained with coffee and chewed on by mice littered all surfaces.

Sitting in the wooden chair by the desk, Sara searched the area. Through a scrunched nose from the stench of old paper and rat droppings, Sara tidied the loose papers, setting them on the right side of the desk. Three books stood atop the desk, but their names identified them as standard pharmaceutical chemist references. The only book in the desk's drawers was a worn leather Bible with the words *Holy Bible* scratched through. Seems the doctor lost his faith.

Sara wheeled the chair to the table and spun to face it. There were five leather-bound volumes atop the table. Sara sneezed and coughed as the dust flew into her nose as she brushed it from their spines. No names had been embossed into the leather. Sara lifted an eyebrow in curiosity, and then her eyes widened. Could these be *manuscripts*? If so, Anya was sitting on a fortune. She scanned their contents one at a time. Two were clearly manuscripts, and they presented reading challenges she wasn't prepared for, but the other three were editions produced on presses—antiques, yes, but not manuscripts. Those were editions of Agrippa's three books of occult philosophy, valuable but not what she needed.

Sara searched the rest of the room. She pulled each shelf on the wall in the hope one might open a secret passage. No such luck. Sara sighed. The book must be hidden somewhere in the basement surgery. She spun the chair a few times, giggling and smiling as the room whizzed by.

As she reached the stairs, Sara paused. Was that shuffling from below? No, it was just the house settling. Sara shrugged and continued her descent.

Sara reached the ground floor and froze. Her heart sank into her feet, and she swallowed hard. Iskra sat on the desk, scanning Boris Skejik's open journal, and Anya tidied the mess on the floor. Her hand rested on the razor blade. In the deafening silence of their eyes meeting, Sara heard her heart thunder. Anya's face darkened, and a heavy frown descended over her lips.

"Oh," Anya said. "Now I know why the door was opened."

Sara brushed a wisp of hair behind her right ear and offered a sheepish smile. "Hi, Ani. I—uh—yeah, I know. I'm sorry."

Anya tensed and pursed her lips. She balled her hands into trembling fists. "I asked one thing of you. We invited you into our home when yours burned. We fed you. I..." Anya's voice trembled with the growing rage of an oncoming storm. Tears welled in her eyes. "I...I loved you. And you made me believe you loved me too. Why?"

Sara raised her hands to shoulder level, holding her palms forward. "Ani, I do love you. And I have a good reason, honest. You know what my dissertation is about, and so many people told me your dad was an alchemist. I thought maybe he would have what I needed. I was just looking for the Paracelsus book, I swear."

Anya lifted the hand holding the razor blade. Her voice cracked "There was a note next to this, a note I wrote for my father. Yes, I know he had already passed, but this seemed to be the best place to leave it so it would be undisturbed until...after."

Sara finished her descent and made a cautious approach toward Anya. "I'm sorry you suffered as you did. I'm sorry you felt so alone and helpless. You were a child, and no one deserves to feel that way. I wish I could make it so it never happened, but I'm glad you're still here."

"For your dissertation?"

Sara winced at the unexpected sharpness in Anya's tone. She deserved that and nodded to say as much. "I can't say knowing that your dad had the book I need, meaning I'm in the same building as it, isn't exciting, but I'm glad you're still here because I got to meet you, to know you, and to fall in love with you."

Sara inched closer with each uttered syllable. Her heart thundered, and sweat beaded on her forehead. Her throat felt dry. When she reached Anya, she extended her arms as if to hug her lover, but the toymaker turned away. A held breath slipped from Sara's lips, and her muscles became less tense.

"Well, at least your house is prepared. You may transport your belongings in the carriage. I will pack you a meal, but it's time for you to go."

"Why don't you come with me? You could see the house. We could eat together. Please?"

Anya shook her head. Tears fell in triplets from her eyes. "Even if I wanted to, the night is falling. I will not risk the curse."

Sara gnashed her teeth and growled. Her eyes narrowed, and her nostrils flared. "To hell with this bullshit curse. You believe it to be true, but you were willing to take your own life. That doesn't make any sense. It's almost like you know this curse is bullshit. And it is. I read your father's diary. He lied to you, because the medicine he gave you—that you continued to give yourself after he died—poisoned you. He made you worse, and you sit here acting like he was this perfect father. He doesn't deserve your love."

"Stop it!" Anya covered her ears with trembling hands as the tears poured. "Just go. Get out!"

Glaring, Sara shook her head. "Fine. I'll go. Stay here with your fake memories, your dead family, and your weird puppet. Stay stuck in the past in your small town with your small mindset."

Sara stalked past Anya, slamming the door to Boris Skejik's office behind her. Anya sank to the floor, curling her knees into her chest. Her tear-choked words rasped into the cold, stale air. "I hoped you were different."

9

Heavy rains pummeled Pazat. The storm rolled in before sunrise on Tuesday and and refused to abate for more than a few hours after nightfall, resuming shortly thereafter and continuing throughout the next few days. No light shone through the cloud-blackened sky, save for the brief seconds when lightning flashed, heralding the oncoming roar of thunder. Standing water covered the town's streets, and the rains sent muddy soil, fallen trees, and other debris sliding down the mountainside, blocking the one road into town. And with storms predicted to continue for the next four days, clearing the road wouldn't occur until next week.

Friday morning, Sara rummaged through her cupboard, finding nothing but dry goods, oil, and peanut butter. She had no cheese, no oat milk, no eggs, but she did have coffee. Her stomach grumbled, and she whined. The heavy rains and muddy dirt roads made getting any groceries difficult. She had a couple of portabello mushrooms and an empty glass milk bottle in her refrigerator. Sara sighed.

"Peanut butter sandwiches and black coffee it is then," Sara said as she prepared her sandwich, occasionally glancing out the kitchen window. She frowned. On a clear day, she'd be able to view the back yard of the Skejik manor. "She's probably up there, eating fresh vegetables from her greenhouse, drinking wine, and shit! Ouch!"

Blood trickled from a slender slit the knife made her in left thumb. Sara shook her hand violently and then sucked on the wound. She ran her thumb under cool water and cleaned it. And then her phone rang.

"Hey, Andrea," Sara said. "I've got you on speaker. I nicked myself making a sandwich. What's up?"

"Clean it well and be careful," Andrea said. "I called to check up on you and see if your house had been repaired yet."

Sara sliced her sandwich in half along the diagonal. "Am I ever ready for some intelligent company, but there's just one problem."

"A jealous girlfriend who doesn't want to share you with your gorgeous friend?" Andrea slipped her words through with a playful tone before Sara could continue.

Sara chuckled. "You are gorgeous, but since we broke up, that won't be a problem. We've had heavy rains for most of the week, and the one road into town is blocked by a mudslide. No clue when it'll be cleared."

"Oh, that's too bad. We'll come back to that. I thought you were dating the town toymaker. You seemed happy. Did I misread things?"

Sara took a bite of her sandwich. Sara wished she had fig preserves, but the store didn't have any. With the peanut butter sticking to the roof of her mouth, she said, "I thought we were, but she's just one of those small-town girls who wants to stay in the past. Her memories matter more than me."

"So, you broke it off. I'm sorry."

"She did." Sara sipped her water. "We had a fight, and I told her her dad lied to her about being cursed to hide how he poisoned her, but she didn't want to hear it. She threw me out."

"Wait, a curse? Poison? How do you know all this?"

Sara pursed her lips. She sighed and shook her head. "I found a few entries in her father's diary when I explored his old medical office and lab. She caught me. We fought. I called her out on trying to take her own life while refusing to leave home because of this stupid curse. She threw me out."

"Sara," Andrea said. "There're so many things missing. Start from the beginning and tell me what happened."

With a series of pauses to bite and chew her sandwich, Sara recounted the incidents of Monday from the time she slipped into Dr. Skejik's office, the finding of the suicide note, learning that the doctor had a copy of the rare Paracelsus text, to being discovered by Anya, and ending with the argument that led to their breakup. Andrea listened, remaining silent, save for the occasional phatic utterance. When Sara finished, Anya said, "Okay, so I get the sequence of events, but why was she mad about you going through her dad's things?"

Sara finished her sandwich and then drained the rest of her water. "I guess. When I first got there, she asked me not to go into his office, but everyone in town called him an alchemist. So, I thought he might have something that could help my dissertation, and then I picked the lock on the door and searched his office."

"So, she asked you to stay out of these rooms, but you broke into them, dug through her things—well, her father's things, and threw what you found in her face? Do you see the problem there?"

Sara lowered her gaze and then closed her eyes. Her cheeks reddened in shame. She clenched her fists and then said, "Yeah, but I was right. I was right about her father having something

I needed, and I was right about the curse being bullshit. And maybe I threw it in her face, but she acts like she's afraid of this curse when she tried to kill herself. Wait! Hold on, I have it right here..."

Sara dug in the pockets of her jeans and found Anya's note. She read it over and then winced. "Fuck! There was another paragraph. She concludes the note by saying she thought about taking her own life, but when she sliced her wrist with the razor, the pain caused her to have a change of heart. She then says the sight of her own blood frightened her. She screamed, and this servant Mikhail came running. When she told him what happened, he begged her not to use the medicine anymore, and she promised." Sara paused to exhale and then slouched in the chair. "And then she locked the note and her razor in her father's office, gave Mikhail the key, and it stayed with him, even after death."

"Seems there was more to her story than you knew," Andrea said.

Sara nodded. "But I was right. I was so sure of it. Why do I suddenly feel like shit?"

"I think you know, Sara," Andrea said. "Well, I'll keep an eye on the weather both here and near you, and if things clear up, I'll book a flight for next weekend. Just think about it. Bye."

Sara nodded. "Yeah. Bye."

Resting her elbows on the table, Sara cradled her face in her hands. For the first time since Monday itself, Sara cried.

An hour passed before Sara's tears abated. The rain slacked and became a drizzle. With heavy movements and a long, languid sigh, she rose from the table, collected her dish and glass, and walked to the sink. She rinsed her dishes and then placed them in the mostly full dishwasher. She placed a detergent pod in the slot and started the wash. Someone knocked on the door.

Sara sighed and shook her head. The last thing she wanted now was company, but politeness dictated Sara's actions. She washed and dried her hands. She walked over and opened the door. Carolyn Ward stood there in a red hooded trench-style raincoat, carrying a picnic basket in her hands. A broad, practiced smile was plastered on her face.

"Well, it seems you've settled back in nicely after the fire," Carolyn said. "Anyway, with the rain making it difficult to get to get groceries, I thought it'd be neighborly of me to help restock your pantry."

She extended the basket to Sara who smiled as she accepted it. "Thank you. Carolyn, was it? Why don't you come inside? It'll be nice to have someone to talk to while I unpack this heavy basket."

Carolyn agreed, and the two women entered Sara's house. They returned to the kitchen. Carolyn took a seat at the table while Sara set the basket on the counter. As Sara opened the basket, Carolyn sighed and said, "You've done wonders bringing life back to this old place. I just brought you a few things, steel cut oats, corn, yams, milk, eggs, and cheese. I was going to bring you some steaks, but I heard you were a vegetarian."

Sara smiled and nodded. "This is more than generous. Thank you. Had I realized the rains would last for this long and be as bad as they are, I'd have stocked up more on dry goods at least."

"Anything for a neighbor." As Sara placed the milk, eggs, and cheese in the refrigerator, Carolyn asked, "Say, do you mind if I get a glass of water?"

Sara nodded. "Help yourself. Glasses are in the cabinet just to the right of the sink."

"Thank you," Carolyn said.

Carolyn rose from the table. She walked by the gas range and brushed against the knob for the back right burner. As Carolyn walked to the reached the sink, a faint blue light gleamed from the affected burner. With a smirk on her face, she poured herself a glass of water and asked, "So, will that Skejik freak—will Dobrianya be visiting you now that you've moved back into your house? Can't imagine that will help with the terms of your great grandfather's will."

Sara stiffened as she closed the refrigerator door. Her words were heavy, sad, and cold. "No. She prefers to live with her memories."

"Oh," Carolyn said. "That's...a shame. Rumor was you two were growing quite close."

"*Were* being the operative word."

Carolyn grinned. As Sara turned to face her, Carolyn switched her expression to one of sympathy. "With that ended, maybe you could start joining us on Sunday for Mass. You've been here long enough to be one of us. You don't want people thinking you're one of *those people*, do you?"

"Those people?" Sara tilted her head. She shrugged. "Atheists? I am one."

Carolyn appeared crestfallen as she leaned in close. She shook her head. "That's not what I meant. You know, *those people*." When Sara's face displayed confusion. Carolyn whispered into Sara's ear. "You know, mentally ill queers."

Sara's eyes narrowed. She thrust the basket into Carolyn's chest with enough force to send the woman staggering back a few steps. "I think it's time you left. Goodbye."

She escorted a huffing and protesting Carolyn Ward to the door. When the farm owner crossed the threshold, Sara closed and locked her front door. She returned to the kitchen and washed the glass Carolyn used. A dull throbbing pain assaulted the left side of Sara's head over her eye. She winced and rubbed her temple.

While Sara spent the week at her home trying to return to what her life had become after moving to Pazat, Anya Skejik spent an increasing amount of time in the workroom of her shop. The rain kept foot traffic away, but the orders from her new Etsy shop continued at a growing pace. Though the mail's arrival had been halted by the mud and the rockslide, Anya expected a new order from F. Schwartz and Sons any day.

On this Friday afternoon, Anya sat at her workbench. Her black veil hung over her face, shading her vision. Scraps of fabric, six unfinished doll bodies, and a half-sculpted head on a stand surrounded her. The lamps flickered as the storm intensified. A cold and heavy silence pushed the warmth from the radiator to the corners of the room.

From her perch at the table's corner, Iskra observed the afternoon's work. When she saw no progress made in over an hour, she asked, "Maybe we should call it a day? You seem *tired*."

"I'm not tired, Iskra. I'm fine. Once I finish sculpting this face, we can head home. Besides, you've always said we should wait until the rain slacks."

The marionette leaned forward and glared to the ability her face allowed. "That was only when we walked. As muddy and wet as things have been, we took the carriage, remember?"

"And it needs a good cleaning."

Anya's gaze had not moved from the unfinished doll head. Her chin rested in her right hand as the fingers of her left hand drummed against the workbench. The left eye socket's curve didn't match that of the right. The doll's cheeks were as yet undefined. The nose hadn't been sculpted, and the chin had yet to be shaped. The antique alder modeling tools lay on the bench's surface.

"If we head home now, you can clean the undercarriage and the wheels. Problem solved. Unless you want to wait until the rains stop," Iskra said.

Anya took one of the more precision carving tools from her kit and traced the desired curve of the left eye socket. "The inside needs cleaning."

Iskra tilted her head to the side. "We placed a towel on the floor to keep mud off the carpet. What's dirty?"

"It smells dirty."

The tip of Anya's tongue protruded beyond her lips as she focused on her task. Her hand trembled, the mental weight of the day's dozen mistakes in shaping this one eye socket. She didn't hear Iskra's repeated inquiries into the cause of the alleged stench within the carriage. Her movements were slow and precise, almost to the point of overcorrection, but this time, she corrected the previous mistakes and formed a realistic eye socket that paired well with that on the face's right side.

"Good work," Iskra said. "Now, answer my question."

"I told you; it smells dirty."

Iskra threw her arms in the air. "What does that mean? I don't smell anything."

Silence hung in the air. Anya's lips flattened and then pursed. Her gaze fell to the floor. She sighed. "It smells like...*her*."

Iskra nodded. "You still miss her."

Anya narrowed her eyes as she pushed the still soft and wet porcelain with her thumbs, forming the cheekbones, which she then filled and shaped with more precision tools. Once she was satisfied, she sat up, cleaned her fingers, and then scoffed at that statement with a hollow snort. "Why would I miss someone I didn't want to know in the first place?"

"Sure fooled me with the way you've been trudging around the house—"

"I've done that for years, Iskra. Especially after everyone died."

"You've barely eaten anything—"

"I haven't been hungry lately, that's all. These stupid Internet orders keep me busy." Anya traced a jawline onto the doll head. "With how you walk into her room searching—I mean *cleaning*—it daily..."

"It's my childhood bedroom. I'm making sure she didn't leave anything she might want."

Iskra nodded. "And the way you sit and stare out the window that overlooks her home and running path?"

With a grunting shriek, Anya hurled the doll's head at the north wall. It hit with a wet thwack. It slid down the wall, leaving a dusty beige stain trail in its wake. Anya burst into tears, cradling her face in her hands. Iskra moved next to Anya and placed her wooden arm around as much the toymaker's shoulders as she could.

"Why does it hurt so much, Iskra?" Anya's words were wet and trembling. "I've been alone for most of my life. I've had no friends other than you for most of my life. Why did she have to do that? And why...why did I think she might be different than everyone else?"

"First heartbreaks are rough. You get beautiful stained-glass ideas of happiness and forever in your head, and then those get shattered by the cold, hard stone of reality. And you're left staring at the ugliness of loss. It's hard, dear, and it's never fun. The best thing to do is learn from it, so next time you don't make the same mistakes."

"There won't be a next time."

Anya rose from the table. She walked to the wall and kneeled to scoop up the doll head. She surveyed her damage and shook her head. This would be another three hours of work if she made half as many mistakes, which was still twice as many as she normally made, as she did today. She walked to the sink near her pottery wheel, moistened the clay once more, wrapped it in plastic wrap, and placed it in the refrigerator her grandfather placed in the back room to store clay and his beloved lemon-lime soda.

She cleaned and dried her hands. With a heavy sigh, she said, "From this point forward, you are the only other person in my life, Iskra. I don't need anyone else."

"Of course you don't." Iskra nodded.

"Especially not Sara Alexander and her soft skin."

"That you didn't enjoy curling up against at night."

Anya glared. She folded her arms across her chest. "Or that sunbeam producing smile. She tricked me with that. I should have known she wanted to use me for whatever would help get her what she wanted. Some stupid book. My generosity, my trust, my love, all thrown away for a stupid book."

Iskra nodded slowly. "It seemed important to her. Why didn't you just give her the book?"

Anya flared her nostrils and curled her lips into a snarl. "Are you on her side, Iskra? I asked her to do one thing—one thing—and she couldn't."

Iskra raised her arms. "I'm not on her side. This might not be a you versus her thing right now. She needed a book your father had to complete her degree. Why didn't you go into his office, get the book for her, and give it to her? You haven't used his medical books and supplies since you hurt yourself that day. What harm would giving her the book do?"

Anya turned her face to the side, turning her nose up at the suggestion. "I might have done that," she said. "But I...I promised Mikhail the key would remain with him, and I kept my word. I couldn't get into it if I wanted to. But she was digging around in his lab when we caught her, so I guess she found it. She got what she wanted."

Iskra scratched her head and then shrugged. "Didn't look like she had a book. Doubt her jeans had pockets big enough for a dusty old book."

Anya chuckled darkly. "Well, then she broke my heart for nothing. Isn't that worse?"

"You're not making yourself feel better. And feeling better will take some time. I remember my first heartbreak. I cried for a month. Your dziad—uh, my own papa didn't know how to handle it. My mama gave me this one piece of advice, and I'll give it to you. Even when treated unfairly, take the heartbreak as an opportunity to learn about who you are, what you want, and anything that may have contributed in even the slightest way to the breakup."

"And what do you think I did? I never lied to her. I showed her every kindness. The only things I denied her were entry into Papa's old office, which I can't grant without the key, and leaving the house for longer than a midnight. I don't want the curse…" Anya's voice trailed into silence as she remembered Monday's events. "She said Papa lied to me about the curse and that I'd rather live with memories than with her."

Iskra offered a single, sagacious nod. "Perhaps you should look into your father's notes and see if she speaks the truth."

Anya shook her head. "I can't. I locked the door behind us after she left. Did I—I proved her right, didn't I?"

"What are you going to do about it?"

Anya's gaze lowered to the floor. After a moment of anxious, searching silence, she said, "I'll just be alone."

The rains continued through the weekend and continued into Monday morning. As the raindrops splashed in the puddles of their predecessors, the fog that perpetually loomed over the town of Pazat thickened in the air. Skejik Toys did not open on Monday. Anya's distractedness and subsequent frustration during work had increased exponentially over the weekend, and so, she heeded Iskra's advice and took one day off to process the thoughts in her head.

After a breakfast of coffee and porridge, Iskra led Anya Skejik into the gentleman's study, which sat across the foyer from the waiting room for Boris Skejik's office. Though he still referred to the room as a study, Boris kept no books in this room. Though not expressly forbidden from entering, both Anya and her mother were discouraged from doing so, as tradition dictated this to be a "men's only" space in the home. While rich mahogany leather furniture once filled the room, the years had led to dryness and cracks in the leather. A billiards table with a tattered blue felt playing field stood near the cue rack on the north wall. A card table rested closer to the room's center. And near the bar that served as the western wall hung a dart board.

The room smelled of old leather, tobacco, and peaty Scotch whisky. A thin layer of dust covered everything. Iskra sat atop the bar and observed Anya's searching. As Anya searched the shelves behind the bar, she asked, "Why do you think Papa had a spare key to his office in here?"

"Because that's where my husband—and your father reminds me of him—always kept his keys in his study. He used a globe where he stored his favorite Scotch, but since there isn't one here, we'll search the bar."

Anya scratched her head. "But there was a globe in here. I moved it into the library and replaced the Scotch with wine."

Iskra sat upright and raised her right hand. "Then, to the library!"

Anya yawned. With a heavy and exasperated sigh, Anya brushed her hair away from her face, rose, and scooped up Iskra. They made their way to the library. Once there, Anya set Iskra on a chair and wheeled the globe toward her. She opened the globe, revealing the wine decanter and glasses.

"Well," she said. "Where would your husband have placed the spare key?"

The marionette leaned over the opened globe and then pointed, "There. Under that glass is a silver button. Press it."

Anya removed the glass. There was a silver circle, but Anya always thought it was part of the construction. When her fingertip brushed it, she realized it was raised slightly compared to the rest of the surface. Anya pressed the silver button, and as she lifted her finger, the silver button rose to meet it. She blinked. Anya tugged at the cylinder, and a small box with a silver key inside emerged.

With the key in hand, they returned to Boris Skejik's office, and the key opened the door. With the office opened before her, Anya swallowed hard. Cold sweat glistened on her forehead. Her breaths trembled as she exhaled, and her heart quickened its pace. Anya stepped inside and sat at her father's desk. She opened the diary and scanned the entries from when she was a child.

Anya's hand trembled as she turned each page. Five entries passed before Anya gasped. With her finger beneath the words, she scanned the page. Halfway through the page, she found the confessional passage. Tears filled her eyes, and she shook her head. And yet, Anya continued scanning the diary. Six entries later, she found another entry where Boris Skejik explored her poisoned nature.

My beloved Dobrianya has taken ill yesterday. Her symptoms are consistent with naught but the common cold, and as such, I have decided that Lana will administer treatment via soup, orange juice, honey, and rest. Should the cold last for three days, I shall intervene by pharmaceutical methods, but I am confident that such home remedies should suffice.

What disturbs me is the impact our child's persistent condition may have upon us. Lana had cut left thumb while breaking down the chicken for the soup. She cleaned it thoroughly, of course; however, while caring for our sick child, Dobrianya coughed phlegm upon her mother's hand.

When I examined Lana's hand today, a rash consistent in pattern and color with that produced by exposure to deadly nightshade. When I asked if she had other symptoms, Lana admitted to mild but manageable bouts of nausea and a persistent but dull headache. Her speech seemed unbothered, but I will need to monitor her condition to see if it persists, and if other symptoms, such as blurred vision and hallucinations, develop.

Anya slammed the book shut and then broke into tears. Between her sobs, she mumbled a handful of short accusatory phrases. *I did it. All my fault. I killed them.* Iskra petted Anya's back with her hand and then asked, "What do you mean? Who did you kill?"

After a few moments, Anya sat upright in the chair She stared at the wall without blinking. Her shoulders slumped forward. She gestured toward the book and said, "It's all in there, Iskra. Papa poisoned me with his medicine. It didn't hurt me, but it made me poisonous. I poisoned Mama, gave her a rash and those headaches she had. Remember when her vision got bad?"

"Yes, I remember," Iskra said.

"That's part of it too. And her nausea. All of it, and she was driving the car when..." Anya's voice trembled as it trailed into silence. She sucked snot back into her nose. In an almost conspiratorial whisper, she offered what to her felt like a damning confession. "She drove the car when they drove off the mountainside. It was because of me."

"It wasn't you, Dobrianya." Anya shot to attention. Iskra never addressed her by her full first name unless it was important. "You had no idea the medicine had that effect on you. You always showed your parents love and affection, and they did everything in their power to keep you safe and happy. They loved you until the end, and I promise you; they love you still. I know this is hard, but right now—"

"Sara!" Anya pushed the chair back and leaped to her feet. She raced from the office, leaving Iskra staring at the emptiness of the chair.

"Hey, listen!" Iskra shook her head. "You know the medicine's been out of your system for years, don't you?"

Anya paused in the middle of the waiting room. Iskra's words hit her core. She tilted her head, thought for a moment, and then relaxed her shoulders. With slight relief coloring her sigh, she returned to her father's office. "What should I do?"

"Rest. Give her time. Give yourself time. Then, you can ask if she wants to talk about things."

While Anya searched her father's office, Sara bought groceries at Karelewski's. With the forecast predicting an end to the rainfall on Wednesday, life started to return to normal in Pazat. A dozen other women, including Carolyn Ward and Lida Petska, as well as a pair of older men shopped on Monday afternoon. Despite the throbbing headache she couldn't shake, Sara greeted everyone, even Carolyn, politely as she filled her shopping cart with mushrooms, carrots, potatoes, corn, apples, flour, and sugar.

After searching for a few moments, she found the store's owner, Harold Karelewski, stocking the cookies and crackers aisle. When he smiled and greeted her, she said, "Hey, Mr. Karelewski. You wouldn't happen to have any almond or oat milk in stock, would you?" Sara winced and clutched her abdomen. "The cow's milk I've been drinking has given me some serious cramps."

She omitted the nausea and vomiting. He offered a sympathetic smile and thought for a moment, stroking his chin as he did so. "I'm sorry to hear that, Sara. We might have a box or two, but it's not cheap. Don't get a lot of demand for it."

"I'll take it. And any non-dairy creamer you have. I don't know how Anya can drink her coffee black."

Harold shook his head and chuckled. "Many of the older generations prefer it that way, or with a small pinch of sugar. Miss Skejik, well, she's always been as she is, so I recollect it makes sense. It's been nice seeing her talk to people around town with her own voice the past few weeks. Never thought I'd live to see that, but since you started staying with her, she started to change. Maybe by Christmas, we'll see her without the veil at the Grand Caroling."

Sara snorted and shook her head. She rubbed her left temple and grunted. "Damned headache. Don't know. She seemed determined to live with her memories when I left. Maybe she'll figure things out sooner than later."

"Get you some aspirin over near the register, okay?"

Sara lurched forward and blinked rapidly as a wave of nausea rolled over her. She nodded. "Yes, sir. Have a good day."

"Get rest. Drink plenty of water," Mister Karelewski called out as Sara turned and continued her shopping.

Sara finished shopping quickly, as her headache and nausea intensified with each passing minute. Her head began to spin, and she staggered. The cart stabilized her. She checked out and bagged her groceries. She returned the shopping cart to its corral and struggled as she lifted her canvas grocery bags from the cart. Sara hadn't felt that weak since she contracted swine flu during her first year of graduate school. Through uneven steps, she staggered to her car. Her eyes blinked in rapid, uneven bursts, and her stomach churned and lurched as he moved. She reached into her backpack for her keys, and then her vision went black. Sara Alexander collapsed into the muddy parking lot.

Another shopper who exited the store saw her fall and raced back inside to get help. Everyone who could raced outside to gawk, but Harold Karelewski called Denis Novák, Sara's attorney. He then grabbed some cleaning towels and a gallon of water from the supply closet, went outside, and cleaned as much of the mud off of her as he could. Sara remained unconscious the entire time he cleaned her, lifted her up, and lay her in the back seat of her Honda. He then placed her groceries in the trunk of her car.

Turning to the assembled crowd, he said, "I don't know what's going on, but she's still got a pulse. That's good. Denis is on the way, and he's going to take her home. I'll stay with her until he gets here. Go on about your business. We'll all know what's happened as soon as we can get some medics up here after either the fog clears enough for a helicopter or we get this damned road cleared."

The crowd mumbled and conversed among themselves. And then Carolyn Ward cleared her throat. "It's not like this hasn't happened before. Remember Mikhail Gonshorev? He had several incidents like this before he died, and like her, he spent most of his time with that freak of a Skejik girl. And let's not forget her parents' little *accident*. And we all know how anxious, angry, and physically sick we become spending any length of time in her presence."

The crowd debated her words. They rang true, but no one wanted to seriously consider what she had implied. Lida Petska shuffled nervously, her gaze focused on her shoelaces. Harold Karelewski raised his hands. "Quiet. We're not doing this here or now. Once Sara comes to, we'll go from there. Okay? And if she doesn't come to in a few days, I'm sure Denis will call paramedics. And before you barge into Garrick's office with accusations, remember there is no evidence. Now, go back to your shopping, and go about your day."

He lowered his pitch but raised his volume steadily as he spoke. A few in the crowd grumbled but nodded before walking away. The rest of the crowd dispersed, save for Lida Petska. She fidgeted as she slowly raised her gaze to look through the rain-soaked back window at the unconscious Sara. She remained motionless until Carolyn hissed at her to finish their shopping.

10

An hour passed, and Carolyn Ward and Lida Petska finished shopping and made their way to Carolyn's house. The twelve grocery bags weighed on Lida's arms as she carried the groceries in for Carolyn. While tromping through the mud, she kept glancing in the direction of Sara Alexander's house. An unforgiving, frigid north wind howled from over the mountains.

"Petska! The door's open. Bring my groceries inside before the foyer gets too wet."

The anger in Carolyn's voice shook Lida back into the moment. As she scurried onto the porch, taking care to wipe her feet on the door mat before entering, she said, "Sorry, Carolyn. I was just worried. I hope Sara will be okay."

Carolyn laughed as she shut the door. She reached into her purse and pulled out a small oven knob. While tossing it in the air and catching it, she said, "Bring the groceries to the kitchen. And if that old coot brought her home, I hope he checked for a gas leak. You know those old houses, and she hired outsiders to repair the place. Can't trust them."

After placing the imported non-seasonal vegetables in Carolyn's refrigerator, Lida poked her head over its door and asked, "What are you talking about? Do you know something about the house she doesn't?"

Carolyn shrugged, but the smirk on her face added to Lida's suspicions. Carolyn tossed the oven knob in her rubbish bin and laughed. "I know lots of things, Lida. If only you knew what that felt like, maybe you'd be better off than living with your brother in that little shack he inherited from your alcoholic father."

Lida narrowed her eyes and sighed. Carolyn was still Carolyn after all these years. Lida finished putting away Carolyn's groceries and said her goodbyes. As she exited the house, she texted her brother Paul. *Carolyn's acting weird. You know anything?*

As she reached her car, a silver 1999 Chevrolet Impala that continued to limp along, her brother responded with a string of detailed texts. Lida's eyes shot wide, and she cursed under her breath. She glanced in the direction of the Alexander house and then over in another direction and higher up in the mountains. As she started her engine, she muttered, "I know what I have to do. Great."

The Impala sputtered and coughed as it struggled along the muddy streets of Pazat. Only the driver's side windshield wiper worked, but Lida knew the way to Skejik Toys. The lights were off. With the rain drumming over the top of her umbrella, she walked to the door and found it locked. Lida stamped her foot, splashing water over her ankle. She looked at the muddy path through the woods and shook her head. The Impala wouldn't survive that much mud. And with a heavy sigh, she stepped into the woods beyond Pazat.

Anya spent the afternoon in her kitchen, sitting at the table. Thin wisps of steam rose from her coffee cup as she circled the rim with her middle finger. Iskra sat in the chair opposite her. They sat in silence.

"So," Iskra said. "What's on your mind?"

Anya sighed. "I guess I should've known. How stupid was I to believe in a curse that tied me to our land? But Papa had never lied to me, why would I assume this a lie?"

"Adults aren't perfect," Iskra said. "Your Papa did the best he could, and he did what he thought was right. I remember those days, don't you? You idolized your parents. Papa was your knight and defender, and you hung on every word he said. He and your Mama loved you. You were their light, and when you smiled at them, the world turned to spring."

Anya choked up. She wiped a tear from her left eye with her index finger. "Then why would he lie? He told so many people when the medicine had negative side effects. Why didn't he tell me about this?"

Iskra shrugged. "Maybe he didn't know it did. You'd been taking it for three months. And he knew it was an experimental idea, so he was figuring it out as he went along."

Anya sipped the coffee. "It's not fair. I've been so lonely, and I could've moved. I could've gone with Sara to New York and seen those libraries—and maybe the zoo. So many things I could've done. Sara...do you think she'll forgive me? I...I was wrong. What...what do I do now?"

Three heavy knocks—the sound of someone using the door knocker—resounded through the house. Anya and Iskra looked at each other. Anya whispered, "Do you think?"

"Only one way to find out."

Anya scooped up Iskra and covered her face with her veil. Three more knocks sounded as they walked to the front door. Anya took a deep breath, straightened her dress, and unlocked the door. When she opened the door, The soaking wet body of Lida Petska stood shivering on her porch with a broken umbrella in her hand.

"Hey, you really are Petska Wetska," Iskra said. "What are you doing here?"

Lida's teeth chattered, and her body shook as she said, "Sara, Sara collapsed in Karelewski's. Medics can't get here. Lawyer took her home. Carolyn laughed."

"Is Sara unwell," Anya asked.

"Don't just ask that," Iskra said. "Let's get her out of the weather. Come on."

At Iskra's insistence, they all moved to the sitting room. Anya didn't have anything that would fit Lida, but she offered her towels to dry herself as best as she could while Anya started a fire in the hearth. Lida turned down coffee, but she accepted a cup of hot cocoa. Anya brought her the beverage and then wrapped an old family quilt around her.

"So," Iskra said. "Let's get back to the beginning. What happened?"

Lida nodded. "I don't know a lot, but I was at Karelewski's helping Carolyn with her groceries when Sara collapsed in the parking lot. She didn't wake up, but she was still breathing. Mister Karelewski called her lawyer, and he took her home. That's all I know."

"Is she sick? She was well when she left here last week," Anya said.

"She was angry, but you two did just break up."

"Yes, Iskra, thank you." Anya glowered.

"Oh, I'm sorry," Lida said. "I didn't know. And I don't know. I haven't seen her around town much, but with the rain, you know, everyone stays home as much as possible. But then this happened, and the road into town is blocked by a pile of mud and rocks. And with the rain and fog, no one can get in."

"But why did you come to tell us this," Anya asked.

"Oh, yes. That. Well, Carolyn told everyone how Sara's fall was like Mikhail Gonshorev's falls before he died. She connected the death to spending time with you. And, well, when we were putting the groceries away at her place, I saw her playing with the knob from an oven and saying something about gas leaks in old houses. I thought it was weird, as Sara just had her home repaired, so I called my brother Paul who works for Carolyn on the farm. Anyway, he said Carolyn wouldn't let him destroy some snakeroot plants the cows were grazing on. And he said it can poison milk, and I know she brought Sara some milk the other day. And I though—I just—I thought maybe...maybe you could help her?"

Anya lowered her gaze, focusing on her clenched and trembling hands. "I'm not a doctor."

"But your dad was," Lida said. Her voice pleaded as she spoke. "He was a good doctor, and you have his books and tools. I don't know about the gas leak, but if she doesn't wake up, what will happen?"

"That's probably carbon monoxide," Iskra said. "Don't know how we'll stop it, but the longer we wait, the more danger Sara's in."

Anya nodded. "I've heard it's dangerous. But you said snakeroot was in the grass?"

Lida nodded. "That the cows grazed in, yes. Paul said it can cause milk sickness, usually not fatal, but still."

"And if she's already weakened from that," Iskra said.

"Then the carbon monoxide would move more quickly." Anya finished the thought. "Iskra, you stay here with Lida while I see what Papa's books say."

Anya raced to the medical office. Muttering the titles aloud, she searched through the books on her father's shelves for anything that might contain what she needed. She pulled *Livingstone's Compleat Dictionary of Diseases and Conditions Afflicting Humans and Their Respective Treatments*. She placed the book on the desk and bent over, scanning the pages. She cursed, as there was no entry under the letter *M*.

Anya's hands trembled, and her heart rate quickened. She tried under the letter *S*, thinking it might have been listed as *sickness, milk*, but she had no such luck. Her eyes glassed with tears waiting to fall as she threw her hands up and growled. Milk was food, so there had to be an entry for food poisoning at least.

Turning the pages back to the letter *F*, she found the entry for food poisoning. There, as a sub-entry was where she found milk sickness. Anya sighed. Treatment options were listed as laxatives, glucose, sodium lactate, or a hypertonic Ringer's solution. Not knowing what any of that meant aside from the laxatives, Anya furrowed her brow.

"Papa always kept his medicine-making books in his lab," Anya said as she raced up the stairs.

Once in his lab, she searched the shelves. Everything sealed had expired years ago. Anya cursed. Anya grabbed one of the pharmacy books from the desk and searched through it. She found the entry for sodium lactate first, but it required sodium lactate powder. A note directed her to the small refrigerator under his desk. Amidst all the amber vials with strange symbols on their labels, she found two boxes of small packets of sodium lactate powder. Both had expired two years ago.

"Dammit! It's the best chance I have," Anya said, slamming her fist into the desk. Something thunked as it hit the floor to her right. Tears streamed down her cheeks, she said, "Papa, if you are sorry for what happened to me, please guide me now. I don't know what to do."

Anya turned to rise and saw the book, a small volume bound in tattered leather. The typeface, with its curvy, f-shaped *s*'s, looked old. It was also in German, which Anya couldn't read. In the margin of the page, she saw her father's handwriting. *When all else fails, in 12 drams of sterile water, add 3 drams tincture of v ruza suspended in aqua vitae and 1 dram sanctified salt.* There were strange symbols by the last two ingredients, which Anya used to match with the correct amber bottles inside the refrigerator.

Anya knew boiling sterilized water, so she began that process while she searched for a measuring instrument. With the water boiled and cooled, Anya measured and dripped twelve drams into one of her father's beakers. She then measured the appropriate drams of the other two ingredients and swirled the mixture as she had seen her father do years ago. It acquired a dreamy color like that of a swirling sky at sunset's golden hour. Was this a good sign? Did she do this correctly? Tears flowed once more as Anya poured this liquid into an amber vial and stoppered it.

"Please, Papa, guide my hand."

On the way down, she grabbed a first aid kid and a syringe and stuffed them into her father's doctor's satchel. She raced into the sitting room. Pausing only to pant, Anya's chest heaved as she said, "I'm as ready as I can be. We'll take the carriage. Come." She scooped up Iskra and raced toward the door to the carriage house. With a squawk, Lida followed.

The black carriage rumbled as it sloshed through the muddy mountain pass, down through the woods, and around the potter's field. It stopped momentarily by Skejik Toys. Lida disembarked and said, "I...I know this won't fix everything we did, but I'll get Paul. We'll go to Sheriff Kornov's office and tell him all we know. Good luck."

The carriage made its final stop in front of the Alexander house. Anya grabbed Iskra and raced to the door. Locked. Of course it was. As she looked around frantically, Anya asked, "What do we do, Iskra?"

The marionette surveyed the area and saw the dog door. "Easy, give me a minute."

Iskra crawled through the dog door. A moment later, there was a click from the other side. Anya opened the door and saw Iskra sitting atop a flower vase standing on a small marble pillar beside the door. She scooped up the marionette, and they began their search for Sara.

Room by room, they ruled out the first floor. Anya paused at the base of the stairs. She felt dizzy. They ascended the stairs, and Anya's head thundered. Sweat beaded on her forehead, and her hands trembled. Anya staggered down the hallway, opening every door until she found Sara lying in the master bedroom. "She alive?" Iskra asked.

"I—I don't know. How would I know?"

"Your father should have a hand mirror in that bag. Hold it over her nose."

"What good will that do?"

Anya dug through the bag and found the mirror. She did as instructed. A few seconds later, she pulled it away. Fog had obscured the reflection.

"See," Iskra said. "She's breathing. You can do this."

"I'm scared," Anya said. "And I feel sick."

"That's the carbon monoxide. I'll see what I can do."

As the marionette skittered away, Anya pleaded, "No, Iskra! Don't leave me."

Anya sighed. Her head grew fuzzy, like when she had the flu. A dull, throbbing pain wracked the left side of her head. Her breathing was rapid and shallow. She grabbed the syringe and then put it back. Using the alcohol swab, she sterilized and cleaned a small area on Sara's forearm where she could see a blood vessel. That was where Boris Skejik always injected Anya with the medicine. She grabbed the syringe and filled it with the concoction she had made.

"Please work."

Her hand trembled. Anya swallowed hard. Holding Sara's hand with her free hand, she placed the syringe's needle against the blood vessel. Anya whispered, "I love you. Please live."

Anya's eyelids grew heavy. She released Sara's hand so she could focus on sliding the needle in without going too far. Anya pushed the concoction into Sara's blood and then withdrew the syringe. She dug in the doctor's bag for a bandage, and when she found one, Anya collapsed onto the floor and lost consciousness.

An hour after the sun set, the deluge that pummeled Pazat ceased. Stars filled the sky, surrounding a crescent moon, as the clouds receded. Sara groaned as she writhed in her bed, cold sweat soaking her back and hair. She blinked three times. As she opened her eyes, Sara saw her ceiling, and the overhead light was turned on.

She groaned. "What happened? Why does everything hurt?" She rolled over and added, "The last thing I remember is getting grocer—ah!"

Sara bolted upright and backed against the headboard as she stared at Anya's unconscious body. "What? How? Did she? Is she?"

"Well, one of them's awake at least."

Sara turned and saw Iskra sitting atop the dresser. Sara pointed at the marionette. "When did you get here? When did she fall asleep? What the hell happened? How?"

"Calm down," Iskra said. Her voice sounded surprisingly matronly. She scurried to sit beside Anya. "We came when Lida Petska told us you were in trouble. Good thing we did."

"Trouble? What happened. The last thing I remember was grocery shopping, and then I wake up in bed with you here. How are you moving on your own and talking?"

"Years of practice." Iskra curtsied and cackled. "Seriously, Lida said you passed out in the parking lot, and your lawyer brought you here. Seems the milk you'd been drinking was tainted, and someone switched on one of your range burners and popped off the knob. The gas has been running non-stop for a few days, so you built up a combo of milk sickness and carbon monoxide poisoning. I managed to switch off the gas and opened a few windows, and Anya cobbled together something from her father's notes that moved the milk sickness through your body." Sara leaned over the bed and felt Anya's pulse. She smiled. "She did that for me? She could've died from carbon monoxide poisoning too." After a brief pause, she kicked her legs back and forth and said, "But for me..."

"I think the two of you need to have a long conversation when she wakes up. Right now, you should let your lawyer know you're okay and eat. You'll need food to regain your strength after all you've been through."

Sara nodded. She grunted as she lifted Anya and placed her in the bed. After a quick shower, Sara followed Iskra's instructions. She informed her attorney she was awake and agreed to get to a doctor as soon as she could. She then ate a light meal, prepared two bottles of water, and returned to the bedroom.

Sara dumped the unwashed clothing sitting in the corner chair onto the floor. She moved the chair beside the bed and placed one of the water bottles on the nightstand. She sat in the chair and held Anya's hand. She was cold, but her pulse continued.

A few hours passed, and Sara found herself doom scrolling TikTok. Anya's soft voice jolted her from the app when it said, "You're alive. Good."

Sara squeezed Anya's hand. "Thanks to you and Iskra, but I think you did most of the work."

A gentle smile crept over Anya's face. "Lida didn't give us much choice. She saw you fall and told us some horrible things. I'm glad we weren't too late."

Sara grabbed the water bottle from the nightstand. "Here, drink this. Carbon monoxide poisoning is no joke."

Anya blinked a few times and then sat up in the bed. She nodded and then sipped from the bottle. "So, I have heard. I guess, so now I know. Good." Anya swung her legs over the side of the bed. "Well, I guess Iskra and I should be going then."

Anya rose from the bed. She gave Sara an awkward nod and smile. When she walked past Sara, the blonde rose and wrapped her arms around Anya in a tight bear hug.

"Please, Ani," Sara said. "We need to talk."

Anya sighed and slumped her shoulders. She nodded. Sara moved to the bed and patted a spot a foot away from her, gesturing for Anya to sit. Anya returned to the bed and sat.

"You were right," Anya said. "But you've known that since we fought."

Sara frowned. "Yes and no. I was right about the curse being bogus, but I was wrong to learn that. You didn't ask me to do chores or pay rent or anything. You only asked me not to go into your father's old office. I let the chance of finding anything that would help with my dissertation blind me to what that must've felt like to you, and then when you confronted me about breaking my promise, I threw truth in your face—not to help you move forward—but with the intention of shutting you up. You didn't deserve to be treated like that on either front. I'm sorry."

Anya nodded. "And I was terrified of facing the past. It was less the memories I wanted to live with locked in there but the one I wanted to forget. You were right. I was afraid, and I let that fear limit how much of me I was willing to reveal. You deserve someone who gives all of themselves to you."

Sara inched closer. "You mean like someone who ran into a building full of poisonous gas to save my life."

Anya blushed. She leaned closer but remained in her spot. "You wouldn't have needed it had we not fought."

"I would have, actually," Sara said. "I would have gone home. The rains would have come. That homophobic bitch Carolyn would have brought me the tainted cheese and manufactured a gas leak. But you still broke out of your comfort zone, which I didn't give you enough credit for doing before then. You always talked to me, even from the moment we first met, so I didn't really notice when you started talking to other people."

Anya inched closer to Sara. She smiled. "You gave me courage. Ever since I was a child, people have shied away from me. They love the toys I make, and the puppet shows, but they kept me at arm's length. I know it's from the medicine Papa gave me and how it changes my scent. But you were always different. You were. I was wrong when I said you weren't. I am forever changed because of you."

Sara bounced and beamed. "And if I'm being honest, I didn't want to leave my life in Nouvelle Arniers to move here. There's not a lot to do here, and the big change frustrated me. I may have ignored how you've opened up before my eyes and taken my frustration out on you. I'm sorry."

They both inched closer to each other. Anya's fingers brushed against Sara's. "And my changes scared me. You were the first person I spoke to without Iskra since Mikhail died. And it was as natural as talking to my Mama. I hid from my own feelings, and I hid from you as a result when I wanted nothing more than to be near you."

"You're near me now."

"I am."

Anya looked down and saw Sara holding her hand. Sara leaned over and lifted Anya's chin with her thumb and index finger. Sara smiled at Anya. "Dobrianya Skejik," Sara said. "Ani, I would like permission to kiss you."

With a smile that rivaled Sara's Anya nodded. "Please do."

Sara cupped Anya's scarred cheek in her hand and leaned in. Their lips both dry from mild dehydration and parched from lack of the other's proximity, met in tender but tentative pecks as each felt for the other's intention and desire. Satisfied, they deepened the kiss. Anya threw her arms around Sara's neck. She sighed. Sara inhaled the familiar dreamy scent of a distant rose that surrounded Anya at all times.

When they broke the kiss, Anya said, "I—I want to try again."

"Me too." Sara smiled.

The night was sweet and swift in its passing. The morning sun pushed through Sara's flimsy curtains. Anya groaned as she opened her eyes. Though still snoring, Sara's arms tightened their hold around the toymaker's waist, pulling her closer. Anya smiled and chose to remain in bed longer.

When they descended for breakfast, Sara and Anya did so hand in hand. Iskra greeted them. Sara pulled out a chair so Anya could sit while Sara made them coffee and breakfast. Sara filled two mugs with coffee, adding sugar and almond milk into hers. And then the seven thunderous knocks against the front door sounded.

"No one should visit before coffee," Sara said as she rose from the table and walked to the door.

Wearing a white tank top under an unbuttoned brown flannel shirt and jeans, Sara opened the door with a yawn. When she opened her eyes after the yawn, she saw Carolyn Ward standing in a red sweater and black leggings. Sara frowned, which Carolyn took as an invitation to say, "Praise God! You're still alive. I saw the black coach outside and feared the worst."

"Well, if you're concern is sated," Sara said, closing the door.

Before she managed to close the door, Carolyn stepped into the house. Extending her arm, she said, "Don't worry. I'll protect you."

Carolyn stalked into the kitchen where Anya sipped her coffee. When their eyes met, Carolyn's face scrunched in revulsion and disgust. Sara raced to get between Anya and the intruding Carolyn. She said, "Get out of my house. You weren't invited in. And after all that's happened, you're lucky if all I do is throw you out."

Carolyn pulled out her cell phone and began recording. "Don't talk to me that way. I know what this freak did to you. She poisoned you like she did her parents, her grandfather, and that family servant who all doted on her. You're lucky you didn't die, but I won't let her kill again."

"Get out of my house, or I will call the police."

"Sheriff Kornov's already on his way," Carolyn said. "I called him when I saw that death coach outside. So, Dobrianya Skejik, I, Carolyn Ward, am detaining you in a citizen's arrest!"

Ten minutes later, Sheriff Garvin Kornov pulled up to the Alexander house. A tall, sturdy man with an afro, a trimmed salt-and-pepper beard, and a slight limp. He favored his left leg. He knocked on the door, and Carolyn shouted for him to enter. He tipped his hat. "So, what's going on here?"

Carolyn, Sara, and Iskra all offered competing versions of events. Sheriff Kornov gave a sharp whistle, silencing the chatter. "Alright, can someone—Miss Alexander, you—can you tell me what's going on?"

Carolyn glared at Sara, who said, "I honestly don't know a lot, Sheriff. Anya and I had a fight over a week ago and broke up. A few days later, Carolyn gave me some milk, cheese, and a few other things from her farm, since I just got my house repaired after the fire. I started feeling sick, and then two days ago, while grocery shopping at Karelewski's, everyone says I passed out in the parking lot. I woke up last night and found Anya unconscious on the floor beside me after she brought medicine and stopped a gas leak in my kitchen."

Sheriff Kornov rubbed his temples. "Okay, so why was I called here on the report of a murder?"

"An attempted murder, Sheriff." Carolyn raced to his side. She pointed an accusatory finger at Anya and said, "This freak with her talking doll broke into this house and slipped poison into Sara's blood. And I called you for backup as I made a citizen's arrest."

The sheriff nodded. "Breaking and entering and poisoning are serious crimes. I agree. And, Miss Ward, you saw these things happen?"

"Well, not exactly," Carolyn said. "But I know that's what happened. Poor Sara had the same mysterious symptoms the freak's parents and dead servant experienced before they died. I did what I knew I had to do for my beloved town's protection."

"Funny thing," the sheriff said. "Funny thing is, I've already got two reports relating to this."

"I knew it." Triumph gleamed on Carolyn's face.

"And both of those reports suggest Carolyn Ward acted in knowing ways to endanger lives."

Carolyn's countenance plummeted. Her jaw fell open, and her eyes shot wide. Her shoulders slumped, and she stiffened her muscles. She laughed and shook her head vigorously. "What? No, no, no. Sheriff, I don't know what reports you've heard, but they're obviously confused."

The sheriff pulled a pair of handcuffs from his belt. "And now, by your own admission, you called in a citizen's arrest on a crime you didn't witness, which you can't do. So—"

"Are you arresting me? I have rights!"

"So do these two other ladies. We're going back to the station for questioning, but I won't use the handcuffs unless you give me a reason. Your choice."

Carolyn growled while glaring at both Anya and Sara. "This isn't over."

As Sheriff Kornov escorted Carolyn off the premises, he turned and said, "Sorry to bother you, ladies. Have a nice day."

Both Anya and Sara released the breaths they were holding. Sara slid onto Anya's lap. Resting her head on Anya's shoulder, they held each other for a few minutes. An unpleasant, harsh smell came from the stove. Sara jerked her head up and said, "Shit! Breakfast is burning."

She rose from Anya's lap but leaned down to plant a kiss on the toymaker's cheek. The mushroom and potato hash had burned. Sara kicked the stove, cleaned the pan, and started remaking their breakfast.

And then Iskra said, "Don't forget, we actually have to get to the shop today."

Anya nodded. They did, but that could wait until after breakfast.

Normal life returned to Pazat on Friday. With the rains finally stopped, county crews were able to clear the road leading into the town. Mail service had resumed. And gossip filled the town following Carolyn's arrest for endangerment and knowingly serving and selling tainted food products. And, of course, the rumors flew about the open romance between Sara Alexander, who was supposed to be searching for a husband to keep her family fortune, and reclusive toymaker Anya Skejik.

As three o'clock neared, Anya Skejik sat in the workroom in the back of her shop, working on a custom order for an Etsy customer. Her laptop screen showed a photograph of a young girl of two or three. The child had chubby but rosy cheeks, a bob of auburn ringlets tucked into a beret, and big hazel eyes. Using the photograph for reference, Anya sculpted the doll's face. There was a small box, roughly the size of a shoe box, wrapped in silver paper and tied with a blue bow, on the table's corner. As she finished hollowing out the eye sockets, Anya paused and stretched.

Sara sauntered in through the showroom door and kissed Anya's cheek. "Hey, Ani. You're doing an amazing job. Mail get picked up yet?"

Anya smiled. "No, my love. Should be within the hour, though. Do you need a package mailed?"

Sara nodded. "Sort of. I know Mister Novák sent copies of these documents to my parents, but I wanted to send copies along with a letter warning them they've got one year to get their finances straight before I put the house on the market."

"Are you sure? The house did belong to your great grandfather."

Sara threw her arms around Anya and smiled. She nodded. "I never knew him, so I don't have an attachment to it. But there's this house up in the mountains themselves that I've been eying from my window. I can see myself having a future up there, surrounded by the fog and the old cemetery." She traced circles on the back of Anya's left hand with her index finger. "In fact, I was thinking about spending the weekend there."

Anya stroked Sara's hair with her right hand. As the strokes turned into a scalp massage, Sara arched her back and purred. Anya leaned her head back and kissed Sara's chin. She said, "I suppose it's a good thing I got you this...welcome back present then."

She gestured to the box. Sara gasped. "You didn't have to get me anything."

Sara untied the bow and then opened the box while Anya said, "I had planned to give it to you eventually, but if I'm being honest, had you not broken into Papa's office, I wouldn't have thought myself able, since I buried the only key I knew with Mikhail."

Inside, was a small leather volume with no markings on either the cover or the spine. Sara tilted her head and raised an eyebrow. "I saw this book when I dug through his things, but it's just a book. There's no..." She opened the cover. As she scanned the title page, Sara gasped and dropped the book back into its box. Her index finger trembled as she pointed at the book. "Is that? That the—that's the *De Mirabilibus Occultis Naturae*. But I saw that—I thought it was just a journal. Where? How? Thank you so much!"

Tears of joy streamed down Sara's cheeks as she threw her arms around Anya again and kissed her. Sara pulled away and shot Anya a curious, searching look. "Have you eaten today, babe?"

Anya thought for a moment. She shook her head. "I've been busy on these orders. I'll eat later. I promise."

"I know you will," Sara said. "We'll stop by Karrolton's before heading home. Yes, we are, and then I'm driving us up to your place."

"Our place, dear," Anya squeezed Sara's hand. "You have your own keys, a spot in the carriage house for your car, and a wardrobe in the room where we share a bed. I am also working on getting Internet service, but it appears the house may need rewiring. That should be completed by Christmas."

A wistful smile slid across Sara's lips as she sat on the stool near Anya. "Christmas in the mountains with you and your weird little talking doll. Are you sure your house isn't haunted?"

Anya laughed. Sara's smile became goofy, and she leaned her elbows on the workbench and cradled her chin in her hands. Anya shook her head and shrugged. "It looks like it should, no? But I've never seen or heard any ghosts."

"But Iskra moves and talks without you controlling her. How?"

Anya shrugged again. "I can't explain. She didn't always. When Mama first gave her to me, I controlled everything. When I had to talk to someone who wasn't family, I spoke through her. She didn't start speaking to me until the August after Mama and Papa died. It scared me at first, but she's been the only friend I've had until you came here. And stared at me with that goofy smile."

Anya planted a quick, gentle kiss on Sara's lips. Sara bounced on the stool. "This smile? You mean the one I have while watching the woman I'm in love with exist?"

Anya raised her right eyebrow and returned to sculpting the doll's head. "I thought you reserved it for a master artisan at work."

Sara shrugged. "Same thing, but that sounded less suspicious at the time. And I figured if I came on strong, you'd run away."

"Had Iskra not guided me through understanding my feelings, I would have run away."

Sara looked around the shop. "Speaking of, where is Iskra?"

Anya sculpted the jawline and then smiled. "I'll need to fire this before we leave, but it's ready to set. Oh, Iskra chose to remain at home today. Today was busy."

"Well, I can always bring my laptop and work on my dissertation here. Then I could help out with the showroom...and make sure you eat during the day."

After the work day ended, the two women split an order of pierogies and shared a vanilla milkshake at Karrolton's. Patrons averted their eyes, but stares were directed their way. Though she had lived in Pazat since birth, only in the past few days had Anya ventured into town without either the veil covering her face or Iskra. The two talked and laughed as they ate, holding hands while sipping from the two straws. An old man at the diner's far end glared disapprovingly from over his newspaper. His coffee grew cold.

After their afternoon snack, Sara and Anya returned to Skejik Toys where Sara had parked her blue Civic. Sara opened Anya's door, and the toymaker slipped inside and buckled her seatbelt. They drove along the path through the forest and up the mountain to the Skejik manor. They parked, and as they reached the door connecting the carriage house to the manor, Anya paused and pointed to the ascending stairs.

"We'll update the wiring to the entire house," Anya said. "But I thought you might like if we converted the apartment above the carriage house into your office. It's livable now, but it doesn't have the Internet access I know you need. If that's not to your liking, we could always move you into Papa's old offices, but this would give you more space."

Sara beamed and bounced. "I've always wanted a she-shed. I'll help get it ready. Having a place to work so when I'm away from work, I'm away from work—oh!—that'll be amazing. Thank you!"

Sara threw her arms around Anya's neck and kissed her. The toymaker's soft, slick lips tasted of vanilla ice cream. Anya wrapped one arm around Sara's slender waist and the other rested against the back of the blonde's head. Anya's tongue brushed against Sara's lips. They parted in invitation. Anya's tongue slid between them. Her breath was warm but sweet. As the kiss broke, Sara moaned and sighed. She smiled as her eyes opened.

Hand in hand, they walked into the sitting room to be greeted by Iskra. "You're here in time for *Jeopardy*. With Sara here, I might have some competition."

Sara giggled. "It's good to see you too, Iskra."

After planting a kiss on Iskra's cheek, Anya and Iskra snuggled together on the sofa as Mayim Bialik greeted the three contestants and the audience. As one contestants mistook rose's sap and petals for the source of the strongest essence, Anya noted that the thorns hold the rarest, most potent essence. Sara kissed her cheek as Bialik reminded the contestants that one who dares not to grasp the thorn should not crave to hold the rose. As the dreamy, distant scent of roses filled the air around them, Sara and Anya settled in for a new beginning of their life, together.

Epilogue

21 December

Snow blanketed the Pocono Mountains, covering the streets, yards, and rooftops of the buildings in Pazat. The winter sun shone through the thin veil of fog but provided little warmth as the north wind shook the leafless trees with its howls. The town was awash with winter finery, as homes and businesses alike adorned their roofs, doors, and windows with lights and decorations. Large candy canes, ball-shaped ornaments, and snowmen in red, green, and silver tinsel hung from the lamp posts in the town square where columns of alternating candy canes and snowmen led to the town hall. And for the first time in anyone's memory, Skejik Toys framed their windows in lights and added a decorated tree with numerous presents beneath it to the main window display.

In the first few hours after dawn, Anya Skejik sat in the conservatory's reading nook, sipping hercoffee while wearing a burgundy sweater, black leggings, and fuzzy gray socks. Between sips, her calm and smiling gaze turned to the scene outside the bay window. There, Sara Abernathy, dressed in a brown Carhartt jacket over a purple and black plaid flannel shirt, jeans, and brown boots chopped wood.

"You're coffee's getting cold," Iskra said.

Anya mumbled something incoherent as she watched Sara work. Split logs fell into the snow with every third axe stroke.

Sara paused and wiped her forehead. She took two deep breaths, and each exhalation produced a puffy white cloud. Anya sipped her coffee and frowned.

"It's g0ne cold," she said.

Iskra yawned. "Can't imagine why."

"Are you well, Iskra? You've been tired lately."

Iskra nodded. "These joints are starting to feel their age. You've kept me in great condition, but age comes for us all."

A few minutes later, Sara entered the conservatory, the flannel shirt unbottoned to reveal the ribbed tank top beneath it. She planted a tender kiss on Anya's lips and sat on the floor beside the nook. She stretched her arms and back and then said, "Well, that should keep the hearth happy for the next week or so."

Anya smiled. "I love the smell and feel of a blazing hearth."

"We'll have to make use of it," Sara said. "Wine by the fire on Christmas, perhaps?"

Anya nodded. "The tree is right there." She sighed. "It was so much fun decorating it this year."

"Yeah," Iskra added through another yawn. "First time we've set it up in fifteen years. Its nice to see life coming back to the old house."

"Oh, I can't wait to join everyone for carols and cocoa tonight." Sara placed her hand on Anya's thigh and gave it a squeeze.

Anya nodded. "I'm not much of a singer, but there is a certain beauty to singing by candlelight on a snowy night."

"I'm not either." Sara laughed. "It's like karaoke. Bad, enthusiastic singing is half the fun. Oh! I'll take you to my favorite karaoke bar in Nouvelle Arniers when we head down for my defense right before Mardi Gras break."

Three knocks sounded against the front door. Anya and Sara looked at each other. Other than Lida Petska, no one had knocked on the door in years. Everyone rose and walked to the door. Standing on the porch was the old woman, Baba, who read Sara's fortune when she first moved here, only this time, her scarf was red with gold embroidery. She smiled, and the fillings in her teeth resembled iron.

"Baba?" Sara's eyes widened, but she tilted her head in curiosity as she spoke.

"You know this person?" Anya's gaze moved from Sara to the old woman. "Forgive me, *Baba*, but I don't believe we've met. I'm—"

"Hello, little one." Baba addressed Iskra. Her eyes focused on the graying garnet dangling from the marionette's choker. "You're looking drained."

Iskra nodded. "The years have worn on me, Baba. Thank you for them, though."

"Iskra, what—what're you talking about?" Anya's eyes widened, and her voice was halting as she spoke.

"This is the old woman who read my tarot cards on the day we met," Sara said. "She knows Iskra too?"

The old woman cackled. "I know everyone, child. We may not have met, but I recognize Lana Blinsky's daughter when I see her." She turned to Anya. "You'd be the spitting image of your mother if your father's nose didn't interrupt things."

Anya felt her own nose and smiled. "I do have Papa's nose. Again, forgive me. Would you like to come inside? The hearth is warm, and we have coffee, cocoa, and whiskey to warm your bones."

Baba offered a curtsy. "I thank you for your hospitality, but I came not for a visit but for what was once mine."

Anya clutched Iskra tightly with one hand. Sara wrapped her arm around Anya's waist. Both women's jaws fell slack, and their eyes widened. Sara's heart beat fast in her chest. Anya's chest rose and fell rapidly. Anya swallowed had. "What do you mean?"

"It's okay, Anya," Iskra said. "You'll be fine now."

"What? Fine? Iskra, what do you mean?"

The marionette lifted its chin. "You'll see. It's time, Baba."

"That it is." Baba reached out and plucked the choker from the doll's neck. Iskra's head fell forward.

Baba held the choker to her left. The last flickering of iridescent light faded from the garnet. Tears fell from Anya's eyes and she clutched the now lifeless marionette tightly, wrapping her arms around its wooden body and holding it to her chest.

"What did you do? Iskra was my oldest friend."

"Ani, look." Sara pointed to the hazy ball of light floating to the left of Baba.

Anya looked, and through the haze created by her salty tears, she saw the ball of light grow into a human's form, translucent but luminous. It was a woman's form. She was a hair taller than Anya, and had similar features. Her long black hair was loose, cascading over her shoulders in thick waves. She did have a smaller, more upturned nose than Anya did, and yes, they had the same warm, kind brown eyes. She smiled at Anya.

"Mama?" Anya darted forward and attempted to hug the specter, but her arms grasped only air. She turned to Baba. "What? What's going on?"

Baba laughed. The spirit of Lada Skejik smiled and said, "I've told you of the old grandmother from beyond the mountains who visits once every twenty-five years, my little butterfly. She visits only those in need of her guidance. On her last visit, she knocked on the rear entrance to the shop. You were getting ready for your first year of school, and I was nervous, being unable to be with you. She sold me a little rose-shaped gem and said it would keep my spirit near you when it was by your side. I was carving Iskra at the time, and so I crafted a necklace for her and placed the gem inside it. She said the magic would start to fade on her next visit."

"Why? Why couldn't it last forever? Why didn't you tell me, Mama? All this time..."

Lada's specter nodded once. "Oh, my little Dobrianya, the rose that blooms, fades. We know this, and yet we still love the sight and smell of the rose. After our deaths, Baba's magic gave me the chance to have more time with you. I became the doll I gave you, but now, it's time for me to rest."

The tears streaked down Anya's cheeks. Her chest heaved. Sara wrapped her arms around her lover after wiping tears from her cheeks. Anya's voice fell to a whisper. "I missed you. I'll miss you. So many things I wanted to say that..."

"That you said to me through Iskra, my little butterfly. I wanted to tell you so many times, but..." She paused and glanced over at Baba. Lada returned her gaze to her daughter and Sara. "But magic has rules. I praise God in heaven for Baba's gift, as I have been able to see you grow from your struggles. Sara, thank you for coming. Pazat may not have been your dream, but we are happy you have come. Take care of my daughter."

Sara smiled and nodded. "Yes, Mrs. Skejik."

Lada Skejik smiled. "I love you, Dobrianya. I'm so proud of you."

"I love you too, Mama."

And with that, the specter faded into the thin fog that hovered at the edge of everyone's vision. With a nod, Baba said, "The day is short, and I've many leagues to travel."

She turned and left. Anya buried her head in Sara's shoulder and cried. Sara watched the old woman hobble away.

An hour passed before Anya's tears ceased. She hugged Sara tightly. Sara kissed her forehead. "It's going to be okay, Ani. That was...something."

Anya nodded. A faint smile crossed her face. "I am glad she got to meet you."

Sara nodded. "She produced an amazing daughter, and I'm proud of you too. What do you say we skip the caroling tonight and stay in?"

Anya shook her head. "I have lived in this house with my old memories for far too long. You were right about that. I...I want to make new memories for this house, for our house, our home."

"Our home." And they kissed once more.

About the Author

R.S. Parker is a pen name used by Robin Schadel, a former medieval literature and folklore professor who transitioned into being an author and a freelance editor. She speaks, reads, and/or writes 11 living and dead languages. In her spare time, she binges paranormal investigation shows, bakes, plays Magic: the Gathering, enjoys coffee shop and café lunches, and annoying/playing with her two black cats Salem and Pickle. She also tries to convert everyone to being a fan of Bloodborne.

Follow the Cursing Raven Books Substack for the latest news, thoughts, and updates: https://cursingravenbooks.substack.com/